"I'm a man, Joanna. A guy who'd someday like to have a wife and family of his own."

His lips brushed hers in a heated caress, as if to emphasize his point.

She leaned into his kiss. Dimly she realized she shouldn't be doing this. They had no future together. To encourage him was wrong.

For the past ten years she'd tried to remain resolute in accepting the cards fate had dealt her. Now was not the time to weaken.

"I've got to go," she whispered against his lips.

"Sure. I understand."

He released her slowly, and she ached with the futile desire that he never would do so....

Dear Reader,

This month, Silhouette Romance has six irresistible, emotional and heartwarming love stories for you, starting with our FABULOUS FATHERS title, *Wanted: One Son* by Laurie Paige. Deputy sheriff Nick Dorelli had watched the woman he loved marry another and have that man's child. But now, mother and child need Nick. Next is *The Bride Price* by bestselling author Suzanne Carey. Kyra Martin has fuzzy memories of having just married her Navajo ex-fiancé in a traditional wedding ceremony. And when she discovers she's expecting his child, she knows her dream was not only real...but had mysteriously come true! We also have two not-to-be missed new miniseries starting this month, beginning with *Miss Prim's Untamable Cowboy,* book 1 of THE BRUBAKER BRIDES by Carolyn Zane. A prim image consultant tries to tame a very masculine working-class wrangler into the true Texas millionaire tycoon he really is. Good luck, Miss Prim!

In *Only Bachelors Need Apply* by Charlotte Maclay, a man-shy woman's handsome new neighbor has some secrets that will make her the happiest woman in the world, and in *The Tycoon and the Townie* by Elizabeth Lane, a struggling waitress from the wrong side of the tracks is romanced by a handsome, wealthy bachelor. Finally, our other new miniseries, ROYAL WEDDINGS by Lisa Kaye Laurel. The lovely caretaker of a royal castle finds herself a prince's bride-to-be during a ball...with high hopes for happily ever after in *The Prince's Bride.*

I hope you enjoy all six of Silhouette Romance's terrific novels this month...and every month.

Regards,

Melissa Senate,
Senior Editor

Please address questions and book requests to:
Silhouette Reader Service
U.S.: 3010 Walden Ave., P.O. Box 1325, Buffalo, NY 14269
Canadian: P.O. Box 609, Fort Erie, Ont. L2A 5X3

ONLY BACHELORS NEED APPLY

Charlotte Maclay

Silhouette
R O M A N C E™
Published by Silhouette Books
America's Publisher of Contemporary Romance

Special thanks to Tom, for his mountain biking
expertise, and to Chuck, as always, for his
technical advice.

 SILHOUETTE BOOKS

ISBN 0-373-19249-5

ONLY BACHELORS NEED APPLY

CHARLOTTE MACLAY

has always enjoyed putting words on paper. Until recently, most of these words have been nonfiction, including a weekly newspaper column, which has recruited nearly twenty thousand volunteers in the past twenty years for some four hundred different local nonprofit organizations.

When she is not urging people to get involved in their community, Charlotte divides her time among writing, volunteering for her favorite organizations (including Orange County Chapter of Romance Writers of America), trying *not* to mother two married daughters and sharing her life in Southern California with her own special hero, Chuck.

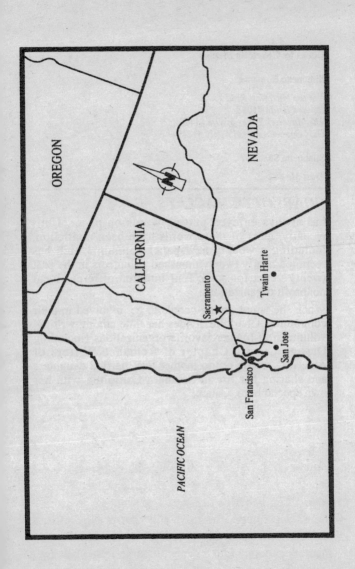

Chapter One

"He had the *nerve*, the absolute gall, to tell me I need a husband!" With a sense of utter frustration, Joanna Greer tossed her purse onto the kitchen table.

Turning from her task of watering the jungle of plants on the windowsill, Agnes Greer asked her daughter, "Who told you that, dear?" She smiled benignly as the water continued to pour out of the copper watering can...onto the floor.

Joanna lifted the spout. "The bank manager when he turned down my loan request, that's who."

"Oh, my, that is too bad."

Tearing off a string of paper towels, Joanna knelt to mop up the spilled water. Given her mother's tendency to be easily distracted, this was a minor accident. "Too bad? It's disastrous. It's already the middle of September. The rains will start in November, and the rental property I thought would turn Dad's insurance money into a decent income for us has got roof rot. The first good storm and it's likely to fall in.'' Leaving her with a huge mortgage on a small office building that she wouldn't be able to rent.

"Maybe if you talk with the bank again, they'll change their mind. Wally Petersen has always seemed like such a nice man.''

"The bank manager you're so fond of is a leftover from the eighteenth century. They can't make marriage a criteria for getting a bank loan. It's got to be against the law.''

Agnes brightened considerably. "But marriage would be a lovely idea, don't you think?''

"Mother, I don't need a husband. And certainly not a husband for the sole reason of qualifying for a loan.''

"Husbands are nice for other reasons, dear. You really should find yourself a good man who could be a father to Tyler—''

"It seems to me we've had this conversation before, Mother. Tyler is getting along just fine, thank you. And so am I.'' Joanna certainly didn't want to saddle any man with the responsibility for her admittedly eccentric mother, or with the burden of raising a ten-year-old son he hadn't fathered.

Not that there were many eligible men in the small Sierra-foothills town of Twain Harte. And most of those who were unmarried wore big belt buckles, hadn't read a book or newspaper since they dropped out of high school and drove pickups with gun racks across the back window. Hardly Joanna's idea of the perfect companion. She'd worked too hard getting her teaching credentials to ignore the importance of an education.

She dropped the soggy paper towels into a plastic wastebasket under the sink. "I was going to run an ad for the rental space this weekend but I've got to go to a teachers-training session in Sacramento on Monday and Tuesday. I'd hate not being here if we get any calls."

"I could take care of them, dear."

Joanna gauged her mother's lucidity. Today was one of her purple days—she wore a purple blouse, purple flowered skirt and a matching purple turban. The gray hair peeking out from beneath the turban had a distinctly purple tinge. Joanna sighed. Her mother seemed quite within her normal range.

"If you're sure," Joanna agreed hesitantly. In order to have any bargaining power at all with the bank, she needed to get the three empty offices and oversize garage rented and producing income. Then she would have another talk with Wally Petersen in the hope of getting the loan she so desperately needed.

Placing the watering can on the counter, Agnes said reassuringly, "Leave it to me, dear. Of course I'll let you handle the final negotiations when the time comes. Meanwhile, I can answer their questions over the phone and tell them what a fine building it is. Right on the highway. A prime business location."

Handy to the landlord, too, since it was only a half block from Joanna's house.

She glanced at her watch. As usual, she was running late to pick up Tyler from Pop Warner football practice. "Okay, if you're sure." From her purse she retrieved a piece of paper. "Here's the ad I want to run. Could you call the paper for me?"

"I'd be happy to, dear. I may even add a few words of my own—a little something to encourage more interest in the property."

"No, Mother. Please don't. Just the way I've written it will be fine."

Joanna didn't at all care for the Cheshire-cat grin that stole over her mother's face. But Tyler was waiting. The husband and wife co-coaching her son's team got very upset with parents who weren't prompt, and they took their irritation out on the boys. Or maybe it was just another excuse for the couple to argue. Too bad no other parents had volunteered to help out the team.

Wrapping the ornate pen-and-pencil set he'd never used in a sheet of the Sunday-morning paper, Kristopher Slavik placed it in a cardboard box. If the set hadn't been personally engraved, he wouldn't have bothered taking it with him. There was little in the office he was vacating that he would need.

Picking up his empty coffee mug from the desk, he smiled. The product of the complicated mathematical formula decorating the cup, when laboriously computed, equaled zero. It was an in-house joke among the hackers at NCC—Nanosoft Computerware Corporation.

Chad Harris, his business partner and friend, stormed into the office and marched across the plush carpeting. Though he was normally impeccably dressed, his silk paisley tie was now askew and the collar of his button-down shirt was open.

"I can't believe you're actually going through with this farce," he complained.

"I've been putting all the plans together for a year so the transition would go smoothly. I don't know why it's such a surprise to everyone now."

"I swear, Kris, I think you've developed a brain virus. You're too young to retire."

"Thirty-one strikes me as the perfect age." Though it was a year later than he had wanted. On his thirtieth birthday, Kris had realized he'd missed a lot of things in his life. It had been a startling revelation, so shocking it was only because of loyalty to his partner and their employees that he hadn't simply walked away from the business.

"But look at the future of NCC," Chad argued, as he had for the last several months. "Our stock has nearly doubled in the last five years, and with this new operating system we just introduced, it's going to skyrocket."

Kris smiled smugly. "All the more reason why I feel free to leave. I have complete confidence my shares of stock are doubly secure with you managing the company. Besides, we've both got more money than we'll ever be able to spend."

"That's not the point. We've got software concepts on the drawing board that will turn the whole industry on its ear in the next fifteen years. Don't you want to be a part of that?"

Kris considered his partner's question for a moment. The possibility was tempting. But no, that effort wouldn't fill the void he'd sensed was troubling him. "I think there are some other things I'd like to try."

"Like what?"

"I'm not sure."

Chad threw up his arms in frustration. "You're crazy, man, but I guess it's your life. Just try not to forget your going-away lunch this afternoon."

"I won't."

Eyeing him critically, Chad said, "It might have been nice if you'd managed to wear something respectable today."

Kris checked his old jeans and T-shirt. They were both clean, which struck him as respectable enough. "Look at it this way, buddy. If I'd dressed up, the staff wouldn't be able to tell us apart."

Chad grimaced, fully aware his dark hair and naturally bronzed skin were in stark contrast to Kris's fairer complexion. Muttering something about ignorant white eyes, he retreated from the office.

Chuckling to himself, Kris resumed his packing.

As he wrapped the mug he'd been holding in a sheet of newspaper, a want ad in the Office Space for Rent section caught his eye. Studying the advertisement, he sat down in his leather chair and tipped back until the springs creaked. He placed his feet on top of the desk, his old running shoes looking markedly decrepit against the dark, rich mahogany. The ad certainly posed an interesting marketing concept, with an unusual opportunity.

He had been wondering what an unemployed

thirty-one-year-old should do with all of his spare time. The ad had provided him with an intriguing answer, one he was surprisingly eager to pursue.

In spite of heavy traffic, Joanna made it back to Twain Harte late Tuesday afternoon before dinnertime.

She found Tyler sprawled on the couch in the living room and gave him a big hug. His face was streaked with dirt, his blond hair—a shade lighter than her own—was matted to his head and he smelled of little-boy sweat.

"I missed you, tiger," she said, her heart swelling with so much love for her son she could barely contain it as she kissed him.

"Gee, Mom, you don't have to get so mushy about it," he complained, even as a smile dimpled his boyish cheeks.

"It's okay, none of your friends saw me kiss you," she said in a stage whisper. She snatched the omnipresent football from his hands, twirled it around and handed it back to him with a loving smile. "Where's your grandma?"

"Here I am, dear." Agnes appeared from the kitchen and kissed her daughter. It was an apricot day—lightweight summer slacks, blouse and turban. Her hair remained an unsettling shade of purple. "I have good news for you."

"What's that?"

"I've already rented one of the offices to a charming gentleman, and he's taken the garage, too."

"Mother, I thought you were going to wait—"

Tyler straddled the arm of the couch. "Grandma's been going crazy. The phone's been totally ringing off the hook about the ad in the paper."

"It has?" Joanna had assumed it would take some weeks to rent the offices, and she hadn't been entirely confident the oversize garage and storage shed would rent at all. If only the Forest Service hadn't decided to vacate the property in an effort to consolidate their facilities and save money, she wouldn't be in such a difficult financial bind.

"I have several more gentlemen coming to see the property later this week, and one is coming up from the valley this evening after work. They all wanted to wait until you were home. But this gentleman— Kristopher Slavik is his name—was anxious to move right in."

"I hope you got his references?"

"I didn't think that was necessary, dear. He and I hit it off right away. I'm sure he'll be a fine tenant."

Joanna mentally groaned. Relying on her mother's judgment, particularly since Joanna's father had died nearly two years ago, was like walking through a heavy fog. It was easy to lose your sense of direction.

"Maybe I'd better meet him," Joanna said. "Did he sign a lease?"

"Yes, and he paid cash, too. First and last month, just like you said they should."

Tyler added, "Man, he pulled out a wad of money so fat I nearly choked. He's got to be loaded, Mom! Totally fat city!"

"A roll of one-dollar bills can look like a lot of money and not amount to a great deal," Joanna reminded her son. Some smart operators also tried to con elderly women with scams that made them appear wealthy when they were nothing more than bums set on separating innocent victims from their money. "Do you think this Mr. Slavik would still be there now?" And if so, would he be easily evicted if he turned out to be a con artist?

"Oh, yes, dear. In fact, he said he'd be camping out in the office until he can find a house to buy nearby. I'm sure he's anxious to meet you."

He might not be so thrilled when Joanna called his bluff. She wasn't about to have an aging Lothario trying to take advantage of her mother. From now on Mr. Slavik would have to deal with her.

After leaving her suitcase in the middle of the living room, Joanna headed out the front door. The heat of summer still hung in the air and dust coated the pines and oaks that formed a canopy above the street. It would be another month before cool weather arrived and the leaves on the black oaks began to turn a bright yellow. The change of season would also bring the possibility of rain, she recalled grimly.

She reached the end of the block and checked traffic on the two-lane blacktop road that led into Twain Harte, then hurried across the street. Her sensible low-heel shoes clicked on the asphalt.

A single vehicle was parked beside the one-story building, an aging Oldsmobile Cutlass with one crumpled fender and a trunk so full the lid wouldn't close. A mountain bike was tied precariously to a bike rack on the roof.

Protruding from beneath the car was a very mas-

culine pair of denim-clad legs, the man's running
shoes as old and worn as the vehicle. Apparently the
"charming" gentleman had only found one sock to
wear that morning, a white athletic sock that lacked
any remaining elasticity and drooped accordingly.

Joanna cleared her throat. "Mr. Slavik?"

"Be right with you. I'm checking a bearing seal
that's leaking."

Her mother had been right about one thing. The
clear baritone voice of the stranger had a warm, mel-
low charm to it. Or maybe all men naturally pro-
jected a certain added sense of masculinity when they
worked under a car.

Slowly, Mr. Slavik edged toward her, revealing his
long legs an inch or two at a time. There was a tear
in one knee of his faded jeans, the denim fabric
pulled tautly across his pelvis and the material cov-
ering his zipper looked worn from many uses. When
a flat belly appeared, washboard muscles visible
where his white T-shirt hiked up, Joanna concluded
that Kristopher Slavik, Lothario or not, was in great
shape. And maybe considerably younger than she
had thought.

She stepped back a foot or two to give him room.

Completing his exit from under the car in an agile
movement, he stood and smiled at her. A streak of
grease marked the exact spot where his cheek creased
into a dimple.

Definitely too young for her mother, Joanna
thought, her heart suddenly doing a staccato beat.
The guy was about thirty, closer to her age than her
mother's.

"Hi. You must be Joanna." Intelligent gray eyes swept over her in an interested perusal that left her slightly breathless.

"Yes, ah..."

"Your mother told me all about you."

Rarely speechless, Joanna tried to gather her wits. "She omitted a few details about you." Important ones, such as that his height topped out at about six foot two and his rumpled sandy-blond hair made a woman instinctively want to smooth it.

"Really? Like what?" He pulled a rag from his back pocket and wiped his hands. His fingers were long and tapered, lean like the rest of his body.

Setting her wayward thoughts aside, she said, "Mother didn't happen to mention what business you're in." His examination of her grew more intense, and Joanna suddenly wished she was wearing a gunnysack instead of a low-cut, summery blouse and a formfitting skirt—professional attire appropriate for a teachers' meeting but somehow more revealing given the way he looked at her.

"Guess you could call me an inventor," he drawled.

"Oh? What is it you invent?"

"Whatever comes to mind."

"That doesn't sound very lucrative."

"It can be if you invent the right thing."

"Yes, well...Mr. Slavik—"

"Please call me Kris."

She ignored his request. "You've signed a lease that says you'll pay the rent the fifteenth of every month. My mother neglected to get your bank reference, names of former landlords, that sort of thing. If you don't mind—''

"I think I'll invent a dual mountain bike.''

She blinked. "I beg your pardon?''

"You know, a bike two people can ride at the same time.''

"Hasn't someone already invented that? It's called a tandem bike.''

"This will be different. A two seater to ride on mountain trails—side by side.'' His lips slid into another grin. "Maybe you'll come for a test ride with me. After I get it invented, of course.''

She struggled with the unsettling feeling he was flirting with her, a rare occurrence in her rather humdrum life. "Is there a big market for that sort of bike?''

He gave an unconcerned shrug. "Guess I won't know until I invent it.''

That struck Joanna as a dicey way to run a business. But as long as the man could pay his rent, she supposed it was none of her concern.

"Perhaps if you'd give me the name of your bank,'' she suggested. "Wherever you have your checking account?''

Two nicely arched brows lowered into a frown. "I'm sort of in between accounts right now.''

Suspiciously, she wondered if that was because he was overdrawn. Given his appearance, that was a likely possibility. Waves of sun-striped hair curled at his nape, looking less like a cultural statement than a result of simply forgetting to show up at the barber shop. Or not having the money to spend on personal grooming.

"Then the name of your most recent landlord would be helpful," she persisted.

He gave that request more thought than it should warrant under normal circumstances. "Actually, I don't recall I've ever had a landlord. Until now. I think I'm going to like it."

"Look, Mr. Slavik—"

"Kris, with a K."

"I have a substantial mortgage on this property and I depend on the rents to make my payments. I really must insist—"

"How about I give you a year's worth of rent? Then you won't have to worry about all that paperwork." He dug into his pocket, retrieving the roll of bills Tyler had seen.

"You're going to pay me in cash?"

"Sure. It's not counterfeit."

Maybe not, but the only people she had heard about who dealt in that much cash were drug dealers. Or bank robbers.

Joanna's eyes widened as he flipped open the roll and began counting out hundred-dollar bills. Good grief, Tyler had been right. The man was totally loaded!

He handed the money to her. "How's that?" he asked pleasantly.

"Ah, fine, I guess." It didn't make any sense to turn down a bird-in-hand worth several thousand dollars in the hope of finding some other tenant with more traditional banking arrangements.

"Good. I'm glad that's all settled. So how would you like to go out to dinner tonight?"

Joanna did a double take. That was the fastest move any man had ever made on her. "I think not, Mr. Slavik. We'll just keep our relationship a business one, if you don't mind."

"Funny, that's not the idea I got from your ad."

"What ad?"

"The one you ran to rent this place."

An odd feeling of uneasiness prickled along her spine. "I'm not sure what you mean."

"It was a real interesting ad. One hundred percent accurate, too." Sliding two fingers into his pocket, he pulled out a bit of paper torn from a newspaper. "I really appreciate truth in advertising."

Curiosity warred with apprehension as he handed her the scrap of paper, still warm from the heat of his body. With dawning understanding, she read the advertisement, which listed her telephone number as the contact:

Attractive, intelligent, marriageable woman with adorable 10-year-old son has office and garage space available to rent. Reasonable rates. Only bachelors need apply.

Her head snapped up; color heated her cheeks. "I didn't do this. I mean, that's not the ad..." Joanna lost all sense of composure. Her professional persona crumbled and she babbled, "My mother—she must have... Sometimes she's—I told her..."

Kristopher Slavik simply grinned at her, that soft,

seductive smile that creased his cheek and brought a devilish sparkle to his eyes, doing something wild and impossible to her insides. "So what do you say? How about dinner?"

"No!" In lieu of eating anything, Joanna Greer was going to string up her mother by her conniving, matchmaking thumbs.

Chapter Two

He judged that the natural sway of Joanna's long hair would be the equivalent of a fifteen-degree pendulum swinging across her slender shoulders. But she was embarrassed now, and in her hurried retreat across the street, her silken curls bounced as if they were spring-loaded.

Leaning back against the car, Kris smiled to himself. His new landlady was a very attractive package. Each individual module—eyes that looked to be a light blue, a pert nose, full lips and determined chin—combined as though a skilled artist had had a hand in the design phase. He could see Joanna's resemblance to her mother and her son, but she was put together with gentler, youthfully feminine curves that were quite appealing.

Odd he'd never before taken such special note of a woman. But then he was the sort of man who usually concentrated on one task at a time, often to the exclusion of all others. Until now he'd never had the inclination to find a wife and start a family of his own. It seemed like an appropriate challenge for a man who had achieved just about everything else he'd set his mind to.

The problem was, though he had learned the intricacies of computer programming by the age of twelve, he had rarely delved into the techniques required for courtship. Except for a torrid affair with a college professor, who had been more brilliant than beautiful—and considerably more experienced than he had been—his contacts with women had typically been either professional or very brief.

From the spark of independence in Joanna's eyes and the determined lift of her chin, Kris sensed he would need a good deal of skill in a game where he barely knew the rules and had never learned to speak the language. He might not even have an aptitude, he thought with a frown. Although by age twenty he had mastered certain pleasant sexual techniques, courtesy of the professor, neither she or his parents had taught him much about love or affection.

That might leave him at a decided disadvantage with Joanna Greer.

His impulsive announcement that he was an inventor wasn't likely to have earned him a whole lot of points, either. Although he was looking forward to their first ride together.

At the sound of tires crunching on the gravel parking lot, Kris shifted his attention to the arriving car. A sleek Porsche convertible slid to a stop beside him.

"I'm looking for Joanna Greer," the man said as

he got out of the car. Tall and well built, he looked as if he had just stepped off the pages of an upscale menswear catalog. Not a single wrinkle marred his silk shirt, and though he drove a convertible with the top down not a hair on his head was out of place. His toothy smile was equally unbelievable.

Kris felt a sharp and unfamiliar surge of aggressiveness and instantly wanted to eliminate the competition. "She's not around right now," he said, feigning ignorance.

"You come here about that ad, too?"

"Could be," he acknowledged, already plotting ways to discourage the intruder.

"Is she a real dog, or what?"

"Dog?"

"Yeah, you know. Women who run ads in newspapers to get a date are usually desperate. At least this one owns a little property. If she isn't too bad, I figure I'll let her support me for a while." He shrugged as if he'd run this scam before and cared nothing about the women he had undoubtedly hurt. "Till I get bored, anyway."

Kris's hands clenched into fists. Normally he wasn't a violent man, but he had to consciously suppress the urge to punch this guy's lights out. Given the surprising amount of adrenaline surging through his veins, he didn't think it would be all that hard to do. "Then it looks like you're barking up the wrong tree. You wouldn't want to hang around for more than five minutes with Ms. Greer." Kris would see to it he didn't last even that long.

The stranger eyed him suspiciously. "You sure

you're not trying to run me off so you can have her all to yourself?''

"Not me," Kris lied, knowing full well the way to douse a man's overactive testosterone was to avoid being perceived as a rival. No doubt the masculine urge to compete for a woman was an instinctive throwback to caveman days, one he had sublimated until now. "I've already seen her. Soon as I get an oil leak fixed under this old clunker, I'm outta here. You're welcome to the lady, if you think she's worth the effort.''

"Naw, I'll take your word for it." The stranger slid back into the car. "Maybe I'll head on down to Bakersfield. There's always a lot of action in the singles' bars. I'll find somebody to hit on.''

"Good luck." The sleek engine purred to life and Kris waved the driver off, knowing it was the women this jerk planned to hit on who he'd rather be wishing good luck.

"Don't you realize you have put me in an absolutely untenable position?'' Face still flaming with mortification, Joanna railed at her mother, who appeared frustratingly unconcerned as she fried chicken for dinner. Sometimes Agnes carried her bizarre behavior too far. *Much* too far, and at Joanna's expense.

"It seems to me the important thing is to get the property rented. I'm sure that's what Alexander would have wanted.''

"My father would not have wanted me portrayed as a lonely old maid who has to *advertise* in order to meet a man." Joanna didn't know how she would ever be able to face Kris Slavik again, much less the next prospective renter who showed up at the property.

"Well, you certainly haven't met very many interesting men in the usual way." Agnes made a disparaging snort, ignoring the potatoes boiling away on the stove and in jeopardy of burning. "The last young man who asked you out seemed quite strange. Didn't he believe in shaving?"

Joanna switched off the burner and moved the pot to a cooler spot on the stove. That episode had occurred five years ago and wasn't worth comment. She'd dated a fellow teacher's brother as a favor, nothing more. And Joanna had been more than happy to see the end of an incredibly boring evening spent in his company.

"Hey, Mom, you gonna go out with that new guy?" Tyler slipped a couple of cookies from the cookie jar and stuffed one in his mouth. "Bet he could afford to take you to the City Hotel over at Columbia for dinner. That's where Pete's mom always makes his dad take her for anniversaries 'n stuff like that."

"I'm not planning to go anywhere with Mr. Slavik. Or with any other man who rents the property because of that ridiculous ad your grandmother wrote."

"Tyler, dear, don't spoil your supper," Agnes said, ignoring Joanna's distress along with the potatoes. "It's almost ready."

"But, Grandma, I'm starved. All I had after football practice was a sandwich."

Agnes smiled benignly and turned the chicken one more time. "It won't be long now, dear."

They weren't paying any attention to her. Both Joanna's mother and son were far more interested in dinner than in how on earth she was going to handle a man who expected her to be *available* for who knew what kind of a relationship.

Her mother had pulled some dumb stunts in her life—like the time she'd tied Tyler's sack lunch to his belt so tightly for a third-grade field trip that he couldn't get it off and had to beg his friends for handouts so he wouldn't go hungry. But *this* stunt took the cake!

First thing in the morning Joanna was going to cancel that damn ad!

But before that, right after dinner, she was going to make her position quite clear to Mr. Slavik. If he decided to stick around, he'd do so as a tenant. If that didn't suit him, she'd be more that happy to refund his money.

As night stole the blue from the sky, the sharp taste of embarrassment still filled Joanna's throat. She swallowed the unpleasant flavor and headed across the road to face Kris Slavik again. It wasn't her fault her mother had rewritten the ad. Joanna simply had to make clear to her would-be tenant that she was not available for the marriage mart. She'd refund his money, and that would be that.

She sighed. Except she would still have an empty office building to rent and no prospects in sight—

including the guy who had promised to show up that evening.

From inside one of the offices a rectangle of light spilled through the open door onto the parking lot. On the porch, a silhouetted figure sat on a redwood bench in the shadows beside the door.

"Mr. Slavik?"

"I'm here." He unfolded himself, and she was struck again by his tall, lean figure as he stood.

"I've come to apologize."

"There's no need. Assuming you'll start calling me Kris. I always get the feeling someone is looking for my father when they call me Mr. Slavik."

She smiled. He did have a nice voice, one that made her think of quiet winter evenings in front of a fire. Or soft pillow talk.

Mentally, she pushed the thought aside. "My mother did something nearly unforgivable by changing the ad I'd written for the newspaper. I'm truly sorry if she misled you, and I'd be happy to refund all of your money and tear up the lease you've signed."

As Joanna spoke, he strolled lazily off the porch and stood close to her. There was a clean, masculine scent about him. Not artificial, like a shaving lotion, but natural, with a slight touch of musk. In the warm September air it seemed to hover about her in a tempting caress.

"Your eyes are blue, aren't they?" he asked, his voice a low murmur that didn't disturb the soft sounds of the night.

"Yes." It was too dark for him to see that now.

With a good deal of pleasure, she realized he must have remembered her eye color from their earlier meeting.

"Did you know your eyes each have about a hundred and thirty million light-sensitive cells in them?"

She blinked at the unexpected comment. "No, I guess that piece of information hasn't ever come my way before."

"I'm afraid I'm addicted to bits of trivia that are not necessarily useful."

"Not everything we learn has to have a practical application," she assured him.

"Hmm, I'm not sure my parents would agree with you."

"There are the great poets—Wordsworth, Shakespeare, Longfellow, to mention just a few. Knowing their words isn't exactly useful, but our lives are richer for them. The same thing is true for great works of art."

The way he looked at her was very intense, as though he wanted to identify every single cell he'd talked about, as well as hear her words with exceptional clarity. "I can see the reflection of the stars in your eyes, like diamonds sparkling in deep pools. Did you know that the light I see has to travel hundreds of thousands of miles before it can reflect back to me?"

She swallowed thickly. "I've never thought about it before." Nor had the knowledge seemed quite so important.

"Neither had I."

She felt herself leaning toward him, impossibly

closer, when she knew she should be running as fast as her feet could take her in the opposite direction. She was mesmerized by the compelling note in his voice, the insistent timbre that vibrated not only in her ears but also in a heart that had been lonely for a good many years.

Calling upon a wealth of willpower, she said, "About the rental—"

"I'd like to stay. If you don't mind."

She minded, all right. Instinctively she knew this man, who couldn't seem to find a matching pair of socks and who paid his bills in cash, was a threat to her comfortable status quo. She didn't want him disrupting her life. But that was exactly what he was going to do.

And because she desperately needed his rent money, she could do nothing to change the fates that were bearing down on her like a high mountain avalanche. In her heart, she knew she'd need more than luck to escape without serious injury. Or heartbreak.

"This is the smaller of the two remaining offices, five hundred square feet," Joanna explained to the prospective tenant. She'd managed to avoid being anywhere near her rental property—and Kris Slavik—for two days. But she couldn't allow the space to remain vacant forever, not with bills to pay and a roof to replace. "You'll notice the office is arranged very nicely, with plenty of storage space in the back and a private rest room."

Percival Carter glanced nervously around the office, as if making a decision caused him a great deal of anxiety. A narrow-faced man in his forties, he combed lank strands of hair over his balding head in a failed effort to disguise his receding hairline. His double-breasted brown suit, which matched his prominent eyes, looked as though it had been purchased in another era. "I'm sure my mother would think this is very nice."

"Your mother? Does she work with you?" Joanna asked.

"Oh, no. At least, not regularly, though she does help me with the filing occasionally. I don't have a large-enough accounting practice to warrant a staff. There isn't that much call for a CPA up here in the mountains. But Mother did, ah, encourage me to rent one of your offices."

"Well, that's very nice of her. I hope you'll be happy here."

"Oh, I think so, Ms. Greer. You see, I'm a bachelor."

Joanna's spirits plummeted. "Mr. Carter, I'm afraid the ad you saw—"

"Oh, it was my mother who—"

"It's very misleading."

The familiar tall figure of a man filled the doorway, and Joanna drew a quick breath.

"Permit me to disagree. As the advertisement promised, the landlady is indeed attractive, marriageable and has a son who is bright, intelligent and inquisitive." A slow, seductive, *smug* smile tugged at the corners of Kris Slavik's mouth.

Joanna wanted to throw something at him. Or

crawl into a hole. "Excuse me. I'm trying to conduct some business here."

"That's okay." Kris looped his arm over the older man's shoulders, demonstrating the fact that he was at least six inches taller than the would-be tenant. "Since Percy and I are going to be neighbors, so to speak, I can bring him up to speed on the property. You know, stuff like which trees not to park under. The birds can wipe out your car's finish in fifteen minutes if they've been munching on some of those late-ripening berries."

"Kris! Will you stop—"

"It's all right, Ms. Greer." Percy smiled at her with endearing shyness. "Since I've met you, there's no way he can discourage me from renting the office. Besides, my mother would be apoplectic if she thought I'd missed this chance. She's quite anxious that I marry and produce a grandchild for her before she passes on. Though I doubt I'll provide much competition for this gentleman. The two of you make a very attractive couple."

"Thank you," Kris said. "I quite agree."

Joanna rolled her eyes, then glared daggers at Kris. "We are *not* a couple! He has paid a years' worth of rent in advance, so I'm stuck with him. But we are definitely not a couple."

Glancing up at Kris, Percy said, "I would appreciate it if you'd point out those trees to me. I wouldn't want my vehicle to suffer any irreparable damage."

"You got it, buddy."

"But wait!" Joanna protested as the two men

started to go outside. "Are you going to rent the office, Mr. Carter?"

"Of course. If you'll prepare the lease forms, I'll have a check cut and brought around for you first thing in the morning."

Shoulders sagging, Joanna exhaled a long breath. Kris Slavik was definitely trouble. Not only had he acted possessive of her in front of a possible tenant, her heart had leaped into her throat when he'd appeared in the doorway. Normally she was immune to men, even those she found quite attractive, albeit in Kris's case a little rough around the edges. Aware she wasn't a candidate for marriage, much less an affair, she made it a point never to lead men on. They generally got the message without too much effort.

Kris was different. He appeared to have a serious case of selective deafness.

He was doing it again.

Joanna clenched her teeth as she showed another prospective tenant around the premises. A newly licensed real-estate broker, Larry Smythe was tall, dark, handsome and far too smooth a talker.

Kris Slavik shadowed their every move. He had on a different pair of jeans today. Not new, exactly—still faded and with a worn zipper—but ones without any holes in the knees. Joanna couldn't be sure, but she thought he had on one blue sock and one brown. Apparently he put on whichever socks he happened to pick up.

With a critical eye, Larry examined the outside of the building and the window frames. "Of course, I'll have to install an air filter. This close to the highway the fumes could be dangerous.''

"Dangerous?'' Joanna questioned.

"It hasn't bothered me any,'' Kris muttered.

Larry's perfect teeth flashed in a smile. "Not everyone understands that even what appears to be clean air needs to be filtered in order to avoid contaminates like pollen and lead. It always pays to be health conscious.'' He sucked in his stomach and stood a little straighter. "I'll put in my own water purifier, too.''

"If that's what you think you need,'' Joanna agreed.

"Looks to me like a real-estate broker would want to locate right in town,'' Kris said, kicking at the old concrete on the back step of the remaining unrented unit. A piece crumbled away.

"I plan to catch the eye of folks who are just arriving in town,'' Larry countered. "Besides, word-of-mouth advertising is the best you can get. And I intend to be the very best.''

"Naturally,'' Kris grumbled. He jammed his fingers in his back pockets. This guy reminded him of all those superjocks in school who had given him such a hard time. Their shoulders were a little too broad, their guts too flat and their brains too small. But the girls went for them. Particularly good-looking girls like Joanna, who Tyler had told him had been a cheerleader in high school.

Larry was the kind who was hard to discourage, too. He was confident of his sexual appeal as well as his business acumen and wasn't about to give up easily. But everyone had a weakness.

In his own defense, Kris had learned as a kid how to outsmart someone instead of trying to outmuscle him. If he was going to have any chance with Joanna, he'd have to keep several steps ahead of good-ol'-boy Larry Smythe. It might not be an easy task, but Kris was both determined and confident.

Chapter Three

Kris flipped his visor down to protect his eyes and brought the welding rod close to the bicycle frame. With a sharp snap, the electric current arced into a brilliant spot of blue-white light. Carefully he laid down a bead that would join metal to metal. The transformer hummed behind him, pumping electricity through the line, and the air in the garage filled with the biting smell of burning aluminum.

From the corner of his eye Kris caught sight of a pair of slender legs and shapely, feminine ankles. Momentarily distracted, he struggled to keep his hand steady as he finished circling the bar with the bead, then lifted the rod away.

"Hi. School out already?" He raised his visor and smiled at Joanna. He'd been so engrossed in his project he hadn't been aware of the time. "Always nice to have my landlady drop by for a visit."

"I heard that humming noise." She indicated the

transformer. "I was afraid something was wrong. The electrical wiring in this building is a little old."

"I haven't had any problem so far."

"Good. With only a volunteer fire department in town, everybody worries about fires." She eyed his project curiously. "That's the dual bike you're inventing?"

"The prototype. I figured I'd start with aluminum, then when I get the kinks worked out I'll switch to carbon-fiber bikes. They're a lot lighter."

"They're also the most expensive."

"True," he conceded.

She gave him an incredulous shake of her head. "Your money, I guess."

"But remember, if this invention flies," he teased, pulling off his heavy welding gloves, "I'm likely to be a millionaire. You know, the Alexander Graham Bell of pedal power."

That brought the tiniest suggestion of a smile to her lips, and he noted how full they were and how perfectly shaped. He wondered idly if they would taste as good as they looked and decided that would be a subject worth pursuing in infinite detail.

"Have you done much mountain-bike riding, Kris?"

"A little. I entered the races at Mammoth this summer."

Her eyebrows lifted in surprise. "You did?"

"I placed in the top twenty in my age group. If I'd had more time to train, I probably would have done better."

"I'm impressed." Her smile told Kris he'd won

her approval. "But I have to tell you, if you had a day job I'd recommend you not give it up just yet. I'm having a real problem seeing how this new bike of yours will be any better than a regular tandem bike."

"If nothing else, it's a hundred times more romantic. If you're out with your favorite girl, you'll be riding side by side and can talk better."

"An inventor who's a romantic?" Her smile broadened. "You definitely don't fit the mold."

"I never have," he confessed. In fact, he'd always been the odd man out—far younger than his academic peers, never allowed by his parents to participate in sports with boys his own age and often at a social disadvantage with the women he met. Being different was a burden that had rested uneasily on his shoulders as long as he could remember. At the moment, he'd give every dime he'd ever earned—something over twenty million dollars worth—to have this one particular woman see him as just an ordinary guy. He supposed that was too much to hope for and hated that in the romantic arena he lacked the self-confidence that had been his mainstay in every other aspect of his life.

Joanna fidgeted self-consciously under his intense scrutiny. Kris had the most unsettling way about him, as though he was determined to slip past her defenses by the sheer power of his intellect. And he was intelligent, she was sure. Beyond that, she was having a great deal of trouble calibrating the man. That meant he always had her a little off balance. She wasn't at all sure she liked the unfamiliar feeling.

Normally, she placed a high value on being in control.

"Well, if the building isn't burning down," she said, "I guess I'd better be on my way and let you get on with your inventing." She turned to leave, only to discover Tyler coming in the wide-open door. She frowned. "What are you doing home so early?"

"Aw, the coaches canceled practice. I think they had another one of their fights. Man, they're always arguing 'n' stuff." He spun the football he perpetually carried up into the air and caught it again. "Mrs. Scala brought me home."

"Thank goodness someone gave you a lift." Imagine the coaches leaving the kids unsupervised, Joanna thought, fuming. Paul and Isabel Currant had become increasingly irresponsible about their volunteer duties. It seemed unlikely the team would make it through the season intact, and football was a sport Tyler dearly loved. She'd hate to see him lose out because of a marital riff between his coaches.

Tyler circled the bike Kris had been working on, touching the newly welded section.

Kris didn't offer any objection, but allowed him free access. The two of them seemed to have developed a comfortable relationship, man-to-man.

"I wish you'd coach us, Mom."

Her gaze whipped toward her son. "Me? What do I know about football?"

"A heck of a lot more than Mrs. Currant does. She doesn't even know what an end around is."

Joanna remembered. Vaguely. Tyler's father had been the star high-school quarterback. She'd helped him memorize the playbook his senior year, no minor accomplishment. "I'm a little rusty these days, tiger. I think it would be best if I left the coaching to someone else."

"What about you, Kris?" Tyler tossed him the football. "You wanna take a shot at coaching?"

He caught the ball awkwardly, then studied it as if it was a foreign object that had fallen into his hands from outer space. "I don't think so, kid. Maybe your coaches will get their act together again and everything will be okay." He returned the pigskin with a wobbly throw.

"Yeah, I suppose. Guess they usually kiss and make up."

A painful knot formed in Joanna's throat. If things had gone as she had dreamed ten years ago, Tyler would have had a father to coach his football team and teach him the finer points of quarterbacking. But as an eighteen-year-old, she'd had no idea how quickly a dream could be shattered. Pregnant, she'd been abandoned by the boy she'd thought she loved. He'd told her in no uncertain terms that a man would be a total lunatic to want to marry into her eccentric family.

Tyler peered down at the weld Kris had just completed. "So what are you doing with these bikes?"

"I'm trying to create an independent suspension system for a smoother ride," Kris replied. "You want to see how it'll work?"

"Sure."

Their blond heads close together, the two males bent over the bikes, talking enthusiastically about things Joanna didn't understand. From a cluttered workbench, Kris picked up one of several books, flipping through the pages as he explained heliarc welding and suspension systems.

She felt like a fifth wheel and slipped out the door without either of them noticing she was gone.

It was better that way. She knew Tyler needed male role models in his life. But she didn't want to get attached to Kris herself. There was no future in it for her, only heartache and ultimate rejection.

As the week progressed, Joanna concentrated on inspiring twenty-eight fourth graders with the rudiments of American history, comparing Indian culture to recent efforts at ecology, thus combining the prescribed science unit with social-studies requirements. A couple of meetings with the principal were thrown into the time-and-stress equation, along with an irate parent who didn't believe in homework, much less the value of regular school attendance.

Joanna barely gave any thought at all to her new tenants until Saturday arrived and Agnes announced the evening's plans.

"I think Kris is totally cool, Mom." Tyler perched on the edge of a kitchen counter and tossed his football from hand to hand. With so much high-voltage energy, he couldn't always sit in a chair.

"That may be so, dear, but your grandmother had no right to invite him to dinner tonight without asking me first." To emphasize the point, Joanna brought her knife down hard on the potatoes she was slicing to cook with the roast that was already in the oven. She had not intended to spend what little free time she had on a Saturday cleaning house and cooking a formal meal.

Of course, she could have refused to participate in this charade. But her mother had become so upset when she threatened not to be at home that Joanna had relented. Agnes's emotional state often seemed on the brink of hysteria, particularly since Joanna's father had died. Grief apparently intensified peculiar behavior.

"Grandma told me she's just trying to be neighborly."

Matchmaking was closer to the truth.

"She invited the other two guys, too. Ol' pinch-nose Percy—"

"Don't call him that, Tyler. Percival is a very nice man. He's just a little shy."

"That other guy, Larry, sure isn't bashful. Man, he acts like a big know-it-all. Always talkin' and telling me what a great mom I've got."

Joanna slid her son a questioning look. "Kris doesn't say things like that about me?"

"Naw, we talk about important stuff."

"Oh, thanks, I'm glad to hear that." Joanna was upset at the stab of irritation that shot through her. Kris had no reason to talk to Tyler about her. None at all. She should be grateful they had other topics to discuss. After all, she had managed to avoid seeing her tenant for the last several days. It wasn't important that her gaze always drifted toward his workshop when she drove by the rental property. She really wasn't trying to catch a quick glimpse of him.

Obviously, he wasn't all that interested in her, either. Since that first night, when she'd turned down his dinner invitation, he hadn't asked her out.

Tyler dropped to his feet and snitched a couple of olives from the relish tray. "I'm helping him learn how to throw a spiral pass."

"Football?"

"Yeah. He's not very good. He said he never learned to play when he was a kid."

Considering Kris's athletic physique, and how successful he'd been in a very competitive bike race earlier in the summer, Joanna was surprised. He seemed like he would excel at almost anything, sports included.

Overall, he was the most puzzling man she had ever met. One minute he was flirting with her, ignoring her obvious desire to be left alone, and then he did just the opposite. Ignored *her* for days at a time.

Meanwhile, in spite of her best efforts, she couldn't get him out of her mind.

Kris made it a point to arrive at Joanna's house first, before the competition showed up for dinner.

A concrete path led past flower beds still bright with fall colors, including late-blooming roses on well-tended bushes. The house itself, nestled among the pines, was modest in size and of modern log construction. A long porch and a picture window looked out over the front garden. Behind the house, a tree-covered slope rose steeply to the top of a ridge.

Kris had the feeling he was visiting Goldilock's

cottage. The house wasn't anything like the sterile, high-rise condos where he had grown up. There was a homey coziness he had never experienced, and he envied Joanna what surely must have been a more idyllic childhood than his own. Even the fresh smell of baked goods wafting out through the open window reminded him of all he had missed. His mother's cooking talents had been pretty well limited to what she could boil on a Bunsen burner.

Oddly, the roof of the house was festooned with whirligigs—ducks and roosters and other strange wooden characters whose arms spun with the lightest breeze. Interesting aerodynamics, Kris mused, wondering if their combined power could be harnessed into a source of electricity, like miniature wind generators, and pumped into the household wiring.

He was still considering that possibility when Tyler answered his knock on the front door.

"Hey, man, how's it going?" the youngster said in greeting.

They exchanged a high five. "About the same as it was two hours ago when you were over at my place."

"Yeah, right." Tyler's quick smile matched the more reluctant one his mother so infrequently displayed. "Come on in. Mom's in a tizzy that Grandma invited all you guys to dinner."

In a way, so was Kris. He would have preferred a private invitation. He didn't like the idea of sharing the evening with a couple of other bachelors on the make. But then, he'd learned a long time ago anything worth having was worth working hard for.

"Kris, dear boy," Agnes crooned, sweeping into the living room. Her long skirt nearly reached the floor and the bracelets on her wrists jangled like a gypsy dancer's. With every step she seemed to create a happy song. "So sweet of you to come early."

"Always hungry for a home-cooked meal."

"Of course. And Joanna is a wonderful cook, too. Have I told you that?" Agnes shook her head as though she couldn't remember how much touting of her daughter she'd done. "She'll make someone a fine wife, you know. So talented."

He suppressed a smile. "I'm sure you were a very good teacher, Agnes."

"Grandma makes great cookies, don't you?" Tyler interjected. "Especially when you forget and put two bags of chocolate chips in 'em."

"Go on with your flattery, young man." As she took Kris's arm, she giggled, a high-pitched, girlish sound. "Of course, my dear departed Alexander never once complained about my cooking. Did you know, he and I once served more than a hundred needy families Thanksgiving dinner, almost all on our own? I must have cooked twenty turkeys myself. We kept those big ovens over at the school cafeteria going for days. Mercy, what a time we had."

Agnes rambled on about the event as though it had been yesterday, while Kris suspected it had been many years ago. But he liked knowing Joanna's parents had tried to help others. In contrast, his family had mailed in substantial checks to ease their social conscience, keeping themselves safely ensconced behind the ivory towers of academia.

Maybe this year for Thanksgiving, instead of going home, he'd find someplace where they were feeding the homeless and see if he could help. He wondered if Joanna would be willing to join him.

Joanna's appearance at the kitchen doorway didn't slow the tale Agnes was telling. The older woman simply kept on talking. It didn't seem to matter that no one was listening.

Mentally clicking off Agnes's chatter, Kris took in the sight of her daughter. Joanna's hair was pulled back, and there was a light sheen of perspiration on her perfectly oval face, as though the kitchen was overheated. Her cheeks glistened. She radiated good health and something else Kris couldn't quite identify. He simply knew she was a lovely, intriguing creature worth a great deal of study.

"You're early," she said, searching his face as though questioning his apparent social faux pas.

He met her gaze steadily. "I was hoping you might need some help with taste tests."

"Tyler usually volunteers for that job."

"Hey, yeah. I can do that," the boy said from the couch. "Can I start with dessert?"

She slanted her son an admonishing look. "I've got to go change—"

"You look wonderful just the way you are." Kris blurted the words without a bit of finesse, because it was true. Her tank top stretched over delicate breasts that were perfectly designed to fit a man's hand, and her shorts hugged hips made to nestle against his. A superb engineering job, he mused. Top of the line. It was hard to imagine her looking any more wonderful unless she was naked and in his arms. And he didn't dare imagine that, not with her mother and son in the same room.

A flush crept up her cheeks as if she'd guessed what he was thinking. "Tyler and my mother will entertain you while I..." She fled down the hallway, giving Kris one last glance of the enticing sway of her hips.

He gave a sigh. Self-control had never been a problem. Until now.

"There's football on TV," Tyler said. "A college game. Wanta watch?"

Kris dragged his thoughts away from the image of Joanna's seductive hips. He had the distinct feeling he was suffering from late-onset adolescence, a randy experience. "Only if you'll explain the finer points to me. It's not exactly my game."

"You got a deal." Tyler punched the remote-control device, flicking on the television.

"I'll just go out and water some of my plants," Agnes announced. "It's been so warm for this time of year. I remember once when..." Her words trailed after her along with the jangle of her bracelets.

He shouldn't have come so early for dinner.

Joanna splashed water on her face in a futile effort to cool her overheated cheeks. She never blushed. Never. Or hadn't until Kris arrived in Twain Harte.

It wouldn't have mattered if Percy had shown up too soon and caught her still in her shorts and tank top. Or even if Larry had arrived before she'd been entirely ready for guests.

In contrast, Kris had an uncanny ability to fluster her. That gray-eyed gaze of his was devilishly perceptive. He took in everything. Her flushed cheeks. The suddenly rapid rise and fall of her chest when she tried to form a coherent thought in his presence. Without even trying, she'd made a fool of herself in front of him.

She'd never, *ever* done that with a man. Not since Tyler's father had told her he wasn't interested in marriage and commitment to a woman like her—a woman whose family was so bizarrely eccentric as to be an embarrassment to both him and his parents.

Her throat tightened at the thought. She had no reason to disbelieve the accusation, certainly not when she considered the sometimes strange antics of both her grandmother and mother. And her father, bless him, had been a bit unique, too. Little wonder Tyler's father had thought there might be an inherited trait he'd want to avoid.

By the time Joanne returned to the living room, Agnes was holding court with her three gentlemen callers, as she referred to them. She'd just told a joke, and the laughter faded as Joanna arrived. Three pairs of appreciative masculine eyes turned toward her.

Her footsteps faltered.

Larry was the first to act and hurried across the room. "You look lovely, Joanna. I've just been complimenting your mother on how…"

Flattering my mother is more like it, Joanna thought, a smile plastered on her face as Larry waxed on about the value of the house and how he'd recently sold one just like it, getting the sellers top dollar even if the economy was slow.

When Larry took a breath, she quickly said hello to Percy. "Are you all moved into the office now?" she asked.

"Not quite. Mother thinks I should have a decorator look things over. She thinks mauve carpeting would be best."

"Mauve?" Larry barked. "Good lord, man. What you need is forest green, not some sissified puke pink on the floor. Isn't that right, Joanna?"

Seeing the agonizing way Percy's shoulders drew in on themselves, she gave him an encouraging smile. "I'm sure a decorator would know better than I would what will work best, and I'm absolutely confident Percy will make an excellent decision when the time comes."

"I'm not sure it matters what color carpet he's got," Kris said. "He's already saved me a bundle with the tax advice he's given me."

That shut Larry up. For the moment.

"In fact," Kris continued, beaming a smile at Joanna's mother, "I bet Agnes would be happy to help Percy out with color selection, if he wanted to save money by not hiring a decorator."

"Aren't you a nice boy!" Agnes exclaimed.

Joanna's eyes widened. Kris was mad. Absolutely mad. Couldn't he see the garish costume her mother was wearing—a wild combination of red stripes and orange flowers that would set any rational person's teeth on edge?

Excusing herself to finish the last-minute preparations, Joanna served dinner. Larry quickly recovered his form and managed to dominate the conversation at the table.

By the time she served dessert, a stress headache was niggling at the back of her skull. Her mother never should have invited all three tenants at once. One would have been plenty. *If* that one had been Kris, Joanna realized with a troubled sigh.

No way was Kris going to leave before Larry did. The dinner had been over for some time. Tyler had vanished into the back of the house, as had Agnes. Percy had gone home to his mother a half hour ago, but Larry lingered while Joanna went into the kitchen to put away the leftovers.

Kris stretched out his legs and propped his feet on the coffee table. He frowned. Maybe he would have made a better impression on Joanna if he'd worn something besides his jeans and old running shoes.

Mentally, he shrugged. Too late now. He had more important strategies to implement. Such as playing head games with a certain hypochondriac.

"So, Larry, what do you think of Agnes's garden?" he asked.

Larry cocked his head. "Nice, I suppose. Looks like a landscape gardener has been at work. That really ups the value of a property, you know. Particularly with an oversize lot like this."

Propping his fingers together, Kris nodding knowingly. "You ever heard of that play called *Arsenic and Old Lace?*"

"I suppose. Something about a couple of old ladies who were killing off their boarders. Right?"

"And burying them in their garden."

The silence whipsawed through the cozy living room.

"Are you serious?" Larry asked.

"Joanna's father died a couple of years ago. I don't know where they buried him."

Larry blanched. "You can't mean—"

"You gotta admit she ran an unusual ad in the paper for the rental property. Makes a man wonder why, doesn't it?"

"I don't believe—"

"I noticed the roses look particularly healthy. Like they'd been well fertilized."

Larry stood and paced across the floor. "You don't suppose there was something in the dinner? You know, you can't be too careful about what you eat…"

"I feel fine. But then, I didn't eat any broccoli. I really hate that stuff."

Larry's hand clamped around his throat. "It's one of my favorite vegetables. The other day I mentioned to Agnes how much—"

"It has a pretty strong flavor. It could cover… If someone knew…" Kris lowered his feet to the floor. "But you don't want to hear about that, do you?"

His gaze darting around the room, Larry said, "Look, could you tell Joanna good-night for me? I'm feeling—"

"No problem, buddy. I'll let her know how much you enjoyed the dinner."

Before Kris could count to ten in binary numbers, Larry had escaped out the front door.

Kris leaned back in the overstuffed chair, smiling confidently. Brain could always outmuscle brawn, given half a chance. Winning was the true test of being macho.

Pleased with his success, he was about to stretch out his legs and rest his feet on the coffee table again when he heard the squeal of metal grinding against metal in the kitchen. The unpleasant sound was followed by an expletive he hadn't suspected would be a part of Joanna's vocabulary.

He grinned. It sounded as if the lady needed help. And he was just the man to offer assistance.

Chapter Four

Kris peered into the kitchen. "Something wrong?"

Arms braced against the counter, her shoulders hunched, Joanna said, "Nothing that a good plumber and a couple of hundred dollars couldn't fix. The garbage disposal just died a painful death."

"Hmm. That's too bad." He strolled across the room.

"I knew the darn thing was terminal. I was just hoping..." Using the crook of her elbow, she brushed back a few strands of hair that had fallen forward and were feathering her cheek. Kris wished he'd seized the moment and smoothed back her hair himself. "Dad used to handle all of these do-it-yourself jobs. I don't even know a good plumber in town."

"I can fix it for you."

She gazed at him suspiciously. "You know anything about plumbing?"

"What's to know? It's not exactly rocket science." Admittedly, he knew more about parabolic curves and reentry trajectories than he did about using a wrench, but he'd wielded one or two in the past. He'd manage.

"Maybe I ought to just call someone—"

"It's too late to call now and tomorrow's Sunday. I can zip into Sonora in the morning, pick up what we need and have the whole job finished by dinnertime. No sweat."

"Well..."

Smiling, he leaned toward Joanna, and suddenly she couldn't breathe. He had effectively trapped her against the counter. He was far too masculine to comfortably fit in her kitchen, so tall she had to tip her head back to look at him when he stood so close. Though his stance wasn't aggressive, there was something dangerous about this man. Or determined, she thought dimly.

She swallowed hard. "Where's Larry?"

"He had to leave. I think he wasn't feeling well."

"Really?" She was feeling a bit light-headed herself. Flushed, too. And she wished Kris would stop examining her quite so intently, as if he had her displayed under the lens of a microscope. He was decidedly the most earnest man she had ever met.

"Hmm. I'm sure he'll recover." His gaze lingered on her lips. "Did you know in the 1926 version of *Don Juan*, John Barrymore kissed Mary Astor and

Estelle Taylor a total of a hundred and twenty-six times? All in about two hours?''

A swirl of heat sped toward the lower regions of her body. "Amazing."

"Quite an accomplishment." His head dipped a little closer. So close she could almost feel the malleable, melting warmth of his lips on hers. "It's the sort of record a man could really enjoy challenging."

So could a woman—with the right man. "In two hours, huh?"

"It might take a little practice to build up to that speed. Slower might be better at first."

"Probably." Long and languorous sounded about right to her. Deep and wet and hot—

"Oh, hello, dear boy!" Agnes burst into the room, dressed in her pastel robe and wearing a scarlet turban. "I thought everyone had gone home."

Cool as sin, Kris's lips quirked, and he edged away from Joanna by an inch or two.

"Mother—" Joanna's voice caught.

"Now don't let me interrupt you, dear. I was just going to take my pills. You go ahead with whatever you and Kris were up to." Her mother bustled to the cupboard to get a glass. "So nice to have a man in the house again, don't you think?"

"We were talking about—" Joanna broke off abruptly. They'd been discussing *kisses*. Lots of them.

"I was just promising your daughter I'd replace your garbage disposal tomorrow."

"There, now, Joanna, dear." Agnes beamed her approval. "Didn't I tell you what a nice man Kris

is? Handy around the house, too. So like your father." Oblivious of the scene she had broken in on,
she reached between them to run water into the glass.
"Why, I remember when he added the new bathroom
in the back. He so wanted one of those tubs with the
Jacuzzi jets. Such an expense! Then when he turned
them on the first time, they sprayed all over the place,
including on the new curtains he'd hung for me. My,
my, I do think the air actually turned blue that day."

The older woman laughed lightly, then paused, her
eyes glazing with confusion as she discovered the
glass in her hand. "Now why ever did I want this
water?" she asked. "I don't feel in the least thirsty."

"Your pills, Mother." Meeting Kris's gaze with a
silent plea for understanding, Joanna looped her arm
around her mother's shoulders. "Would you like me
to help you find them?"

"No, no. You stay here and entertain your young
man. I'll be fine."

"I was about to leave anyway, Agnes. But I'll be
back tomorrow to fix the disposal." He bent to place
a soft kiss on her forehead. "Thanks for inviting me
to dinner."

"You're welcome, dear boy. Anytime at all."

An ache swelled in Joanna's chest. Not every man
would have been so kind to a dotty old woman.
Joanna hated the fact that Kris's thoughtful gesture
made her feel all weepy and wanting some of those
hundred and twenty-six kisses for herself.

Household Plumbing Repairs Made Easy.
The softcover book lay open on the kitchen

counter. Under the sink, Kris was twisted around like a pretzel, a position he'd maintained for the better part of the afternoon.

He grunted.

Joanna rolled her eyes. "Why don't we just leave it for now? Tomorrow I'll call—"

"No, I've almost got it."

Stubborn man, she thought with a grimace. "The pipes are probably badly corroded. The disposal hasn't been replaced in years."

"The book says that's not a problem." Another grunt. "One more squirt of this Magic Wrench compound and it's sure to break loose."

Break being the operative word, Joanna decided worriedly.

The wrench clattered. Kris swore, muttering, "Geez, this stuff stinks." He squirmed out from under the sink and held up the old disposal as if it was a trophy. Black goo dripped onto his white T-shirt.

"Wait a minute. I'll get a bucket." Joanna hurried to the broom closet to retrieve a plastic pail.

With a maximum of ceremony, he dropped the grimy appliance into the pail, then grinned at her with endearing little-boy enthusiasm, as if he had won his very first Olympic gold medal. "Bet you thought I wouldn't be able to get that sucker out, didn't you?"

"A doubt or two did cross my mind," she conceded. Odd how powerfully he affected her—in some very basic way—when at the same time he seemed to need a keeper almost as much as her mother did. "If you don't mind, I'll put off judgment of your journeyman plumbing skills until I see if you can get the new disposal installed.''

"Oh ye of little faith!" he mocked. He ripped open the box that contained the new disposal and pulled out a sheaf of papers. "It comes with instructions so simple a five-year-old could understand them."

That would have been true, she agreed two hours later—assuming the instructions had been written by an individual versed in English, not Japanese. The translation definitely added new meaning to the phrase "international understanding."

They'd just enjoyed a celebratory flick of the switch that set the disposal humming pleasantly when Tyler trudged into the house.

"The coaches quit! This time it's for real." He jammed his hands into his pockets. "The whole season's totally out the window."

"Ah, honey." Joanna tried to reassure her son with a hug, but he ducked away from her. "They've quit before."

"This time Paul's moved out. He's gone to Oakland. And Cody says he and his mom are going to go visit her folks in L.A. They might not come back."

That sounded serious. "Maybe someone else will step forward to coach the team. The season's half over. It can't be all that hard—"

"Who? We've gone through this before. Everybody's got an excuse. Half of the guys are like me and don't even have a dad. The rest of 'em have fathers that either work in San Francisco and are only here on the weekends, or they don't give a—"

"I work here."

In unison, both Joanna and Tyler turned toward Kris.

He lifted his shoulders in an easy shrug. "How hard can it be to coach a football team? You boys know all the rules, don't you?"

Tyler scowled. "Well, yeah, but—"

"Your mother can provide the intuitive stuff—like how to motivate the players—and I'll take care of the strategy and training regimen." He glanced at Joanna. "Tyler has been showing me enough that I'm sure I can catch on."

"You want me to..." Joanna shook her head. "I'm teaching full-time. I've got lessons to plan, papers to grade..." A mother who increasingly needed extra attention.

"Of course, I'm busy on Monday and Thursday evenings, but afternoon practice is okay," Kris added, as if Joanna hadn't spoken.

"What are you doing on Mondays and Thursdays?" she asked, as if that made any difference. It wasn't her concern, and she wasn't about to sign on as coach.

"I'm in training for the Twain Harte volunteer fire department." That sexy grin creased his cheek, making him look so proud she thought he might burst with it. "When I was three, I told my mother I wanted to be a fireman. She didn't exactly approve, so I changed my career goal. I figure she'll be furious when she learns that I'm going to get my way, after all. She'll have an even worse cardiac attack when I tell her I'm coaching a football team. She hates sports.''

Joanna knew she shouldn't agree to help Kris anger his mother. But he was so excited about the prospect, so full of himself, how could she refuse? Besides, Tyler really did love football. It wouldn't be fair if she turned down the volunteer coaching job and her son missed the rest of the season.

"Okay," she agreed. "I'll help coach the team. But, don't you dare blame me if we end up in the cellar."

"Not a chance, Mom. The guys will be so psyched having a hot lady like you coaching, they'll want to show off their stuff."

"Tyler!"

Kris's warm, mocking laughter accompanied Tyler's escape from the kitchen, making Joanna wonder what on earth she had gotten herself into. She'd intended to sacrifice a certain amount of her free time to help out her son. Clearly she hadn't given enough thought to how coaching his team would throw her into frequent contact with the one man she knew she should avoid.

"All right, gentlemen," Kris ordered. "Twice around the track at a jog and then we'll do some stretching exercises."

"Twice!" the gaggle of boys in shoulder pads complained.

"The Currants only made us do one lap," a boy with a buzz cut argued.

"We wanna play football, not run track," a heavy-set youngster added.

"Yeah," they agreed in unison.

Wearing running shorts and an old T-shirt, Kris juggled the armload of books he'd carried onto the field. As he thumbed through the pages of one, two others dropped to the ground. Joanna bent to retrieve them, her gaze drifting unobtrusively to admire muscular legs lightly roughened with sandy-blond hair.

"It says here in *Successful Coaching,*" Kris replied, "that conditioning is the key to winning. The fourth quarter is when games are really won and lost. The team with the greatest overall endurance—"

"Aw, gee!" the boys chorused.

"Boys..." Joanna said in her patient teacher voice. "Either Mr. Slavik and I are your coaches, and you do what we say, or your football season is over for the year. It's your choice."

The grumbling subsided as, one after the other, the players gave in, turned and jogged toward the end of the field.

Kris shoved the rest of the books into Joanna's hands. "Hold these, would you? I'll be back in a minute."

"Where are you going?"

"I'm doing laps. A good leader never asks his troops to do anything he isn't willing to do."

"Did that come from these books, too?"

He grinned at her. "Nope. That's common sense."

Setting off at a run, he soon caught up with the back of the pack as his long, easy strides gobbled up the distance. Immediately he cajoled the laggers into picking up the pace. To Joanna's surprise, even the least athletic of the boys increased his effort. Soon the whole team looked like a well-oiled machine working together as they rounded the field.

Barely giving them a chance to catch their breaths following the second lap, Kris had the team doing stretching exercises. Then he divided them into offensive and defensive units to practice their standard plays, instinctively selecting the natural leaders to organize the drills.

He came to the side of the field where Joanna had been observing and stood beside her. His hair looked mussed and damp with perspiration; a V of sweat stained his T-shirt.

"So what do you think?" he asked, appearing not in the least out of breath.

"I'm impressed. It took you less than five minutes to whip those boys into shape. I think you don't need me around at all."

"You're wrong about that. How do you think I got those guys to run so hard?"

"I don't know. By being a good role model, I suppose."

"Nope." A smile creased his cheek and his gray eyes twinkled with mischief. "I told 'em you used to be a high-school cheerleader, and I promised if they won the league you'd wear one of those short skirts and do a back flip—"

"You did what?" she sputtered. "It's been years since I..." The sparkle in his eyes grew even brighter and more suspicious. "You're teasing me, right?"

"Well, maybe I just told 'em I'd treat for pizza if

they won.'' He shrugged. ''But I wouldn't mind seeing you in a short skirt. I bet you were sensational
as a cheerleader.''

''That was a long time ago.'' In another lifetime,
before she'd learned dreams could shatter.

He eyed her appreciatively, his gaze traveling
slowly from her face clear down to her toes and lei-
surely back up again, heating every inch of her body
as he skimmed over her. ''You look like it could
have been yesterday.''

''Yes, well…'' She cleared the odd constriction
from her throat with the same determination she
tamped down an old dream that threatened to reap-
pear. ''Shouldn't we be watching the boys?''

''I have been. I want to change number seven to
a wide receiver. He's quick but he's not tall enough
for a defensive back. If he's got good hands, he'll be
better on offense.''

How had Kris reached that decision, she wondered, when it appeared he'd been fully concentrat-
ing on her? In contrast, she'd been totally absorbed
with him. She couldn't have told anyone what plays
the boys were running, or even what game they'd
been playing, much less come to any verdict on their
skills. But she had noted in some detail the attractive
squint lines at the corners of Kris's eyes and how
they added character to his face. She'd paid more
attention to the way his very kissable lips moved
when he spoke than she had to what was happening
on the field.

Apparently, coaching football required a far

greater degree of skill and split concentration than she had realized.

Kris gestured across the field. "Who's that youngster sitting alone over there?"

"That's Peter Ashford, a friend of Tyler's, and of all the boys, really. He's legally blind, something about too much oxygen at birth. His parents have always insisted on mainstreaming him in school, and he does very well."

Kris's forehead furrowed. "He comes to football practice even though he can't play? Or even see what's going on?"

"He doesn't like to be left out, and he loves sports. One of his friends probably brought him to practice after school, and then they'll walk home together. During a game he's the team's biggest fan. He knows exactly what's going on just by the sounds he hears. It's amazing."

"I think I like that boy," Kris said thoughtfully. He wandered back onto the playing field, making suggestions to the boys and encouraging them. He'd never been challenged by any disability, and he admired young Peter Ashford's grit. If Kris gave it some thought, perhaps he'd come up with a way to help him. Not that the boy wasn't getting along well enough on his own.

In a similar way, he admired Joanna's success in raising her son alone. Clearly Tyler was a natural leader, well liked, and talented in athletics. He appeared amazingly well adjusted for a youngster who had never known his father. That, Kris concluded, spoke volumes about his mother.

He checked over his shoulder to find the woman in question in a three-point stance coaching a couple of linemen who were half her size. She had the decidedly more attractive tush, however. In that position, her cotton shorts clung to her derriere like a body glove. Gentleman that he was, Kris resisted the impulse to join her and run his hand over the smooth shape that he found so appealing.

By the time practice was over, all of the boys looked thoroughly bedraggled, Tyler included. Joanna gave him a quick hug.

"You look beat, tiger."

"I'm okay." He sidestepped away, presumably so his friends wouldn't notice her affectionate gesture.

She let her hand fall to her side. Her son was growing up so fast it hurt. Before she knew what was happening, he'd be off on his own. And she'd be alone, except for her mother. Until now that prospect hadn't seemed so terrible. Slipping Kris a glance, she wondered what had changed.

"Hey, Kris, you're coming to dinner tonight, aren't you?" Tyler asked as the three of them walked toward the parking lot.

"Honey, Kris volunteered to coach your team. That doesn't mean he wants to hang around with you full-time. He has his own life to lead." And so did she.

"Actually..." Kris stopped by his car, a sheepish look on his face. "I sort of hinted to Agnes that I really like corn beef and cabbage. I think it's on the menu tonight."

"Oh." Joanna gritted her teeth. She'd been outmaneuvered again by her matchmaking mother. It would hardly be gracious to tell Kris he couldn't come to dinner when he'd done such a good job of coaching her son's team this afternoon. A man had to eat, didn't he? Providing him with a meal or two seemed small thanks for all of his efforts.

It was her persistent reaction to Kris that troubled Joanna far more than the simple act of breaking bread with him. She had no right to want the things he made her think about. If he knew the truth about her entire family and their frequently bizarre behavior, he would probably run the opposite direction as fast as his long, muscular legs would take him.

Tyler's biological father had certainly reacted that way.

When Joanna fled to her room after dinner, pleading—probably truthfully—that she had school papers to grade, Kris accepted Tyler's invitation to check out his computer games. Joanna's son had no way of knowing Kris had practically teethed on computer games far more complicated than those the youngster had in his small library. In fact, the newest generation of virtual-reality programs had been based on one of Kris's concepts.

Kris pulled up a second chair in front of the boy's computer.

"So there's this guy," Tyler explained as he booted up the program. "He's inside an empty warehouse or something, and these aliens are after him. You've got weapons and ammo, and your fist if you run out of the big stuff, and you're suppose to blow these alien dudes away before they get you."

"Sounds a little violent," Kris commented. He knew the game the boy was talking about—a decidedly uninspired concept as far as he was concerned.

"Yeah, Mom hates it. She only buys me the educational stuff. But one of my buddies let me make a copy of this one. It's totally rad, man."

"Right." It was also probably a bootlegged program, made in violation of copyright laws. Not an unusual occurrence in the industry but discouraging for the creator, who didn't receive a dime for his efforts, however amateurish they might have been.

A screen dominated by a large gun came into focus. After a few basic instructions, Tyler let Kris go first. It took him only moments to master the program—and destroy all the aliens who were lurking in the warehouse. Kris didn't view that as a great accomplishment.

"Wow! You wiped 'em out faster than anybody I've ever seen!" Tyler exclaimed.

"It's a pretty simple program, really," Kris said. "I've kind of played similar games before. That gave me a leg up."

"Yeah, I guess."

Kris hadn't really intended to show off or discourage the boy, but clearly his comments hadn't been well received. "The truth is, a computer, even one this old, has a lot of capacity this particular program didn't begin to tap. Maybe I can get you another game that's a little more challenging."

"Really? Can you do that?"

He shrugged. "Sure. If that's what you'd like."

"Well, yeah, but..." Tyler's expression clouded, a reflection of a young man being pricked by his conscience. "Mom doesn't exactly approve of me using her computer for games 'n' stuff. She'd rather I use it for homework and researching papers. In fact, she'd like to have enough computers in her class-room to get all of her kids on-line. She's always talk-ing about the power of computers as an educational tool, but the school board won't cut loose any money for the hardware."

"There aren't any computers in her classroom?" Kris asked, appalled. Every child ought to have ac-cess to technology just as much as every kid needed to have a pencil.

"I guess she can get a couple from the science teacher when she needs them for a special project or something. But that's all."

Not good enough, Kris thought. Twain Harte was now his hometown. He didn't like the idea that the local students were missing a large part of their ed-ucation simply because of a lack of funds.

Money wasn't a problem for him. Neither was ac-cess to a whole warehouse full of surplus equipment.

What was far more difficult, given his limited ex-perience, was to successfully court a woman who appeared reluctant. Joanna's disinclination to fully embrace his pursuit nagged at him. In the computer arena he was a can-do guy; with Joanna he was far less sure of himself.

Chapter Five

The classroom door opened and the principal peeked in, the shine of his bald head preceding him by a scant millisecond. "May I see you, Ms. Greer?"

"Of course." Joanna turned to her room full of fourth graders, each of whom had glanced up at the sound of the principal's voice. In general, Mr. Murdock's arrival meant trouble, though she couldn't imagine what the problem might be now. "Continue copying what's on the board," she told her students, "and then open your books to page thirty-six and begin reading. I'll be right back."

She stepped into the hallway.

"Ms. Greer, there's a delivery truck outside," the principal began. "The driver indicates he has about fifty computers for our school, ten of which he is directed to install in your classroom."

"Computers? For my classroom?"

"Yes. They're from some company named Nanosoft Computerware. Do you know anything about this?''

She shook her head. "Not a thing. It was my understanding the school board had nixed any more computers for now.'' A decision they made year after year in spite of continuing requests from the teachers.

"Indeed they have. According to the young man, these are contributions. There's to be no charge to the school district.''

"Why, that's wonderful!'' Rather like the arrival of Santa Claus in October. "Are you sure there isn't some kind of a hitch?''

"After consulting with the superintendent, we've decided to accept the contribution, assuming we have adequate assurances no costs will be incurred by the district. It will mean, however, that there will be some disruption in your classes.''

"Oh? Why's that?''

"The young man has been instructed to see to the installation of the machines and bring them on-line. He refuses to simply drop them off, as I have suggested. He insists he's been ordered to remain here until the entire job is completed.''

Good for Nanosoft, whoever the heck they were. Obviously they knew there was no one at the school with either the skills or time to hook up a computer from scratch. "I'll be happy to accommodate my schedule to the installer's needs, Mr. Murdock.'' She'd do whatever it took for her pupils to prepare themselves for the twenty-first century. "I'm sure the students will be delighted.'' Personally, she felt the entire school owed the donor a huge debt of gratitude.

"Very well, Ms. Greer." With a troubled shake of his head, he ran his palm over the top of his bald dome. "Though I do wish I knew the source of these machines and how they came to be contributed. I don't like surprises. It's very unsettling to everyone involved."

Almost as puzzled by this unexpected occurrence as the principal, Joanna returned to her class. The moment she stepped into the room her mind flashed to the memory of Tyler playing his computer games with Kris three nights ago. They'd stayed closeted together for some time while she had distracted herself by scoring test papers.

She frowned, an eerie suspicion prickling along her spine. Surely Kris had no connection to this huge contribution of computers to her school. He wouldn't have a reason to do that. Nor would a man who wore holey shoes and drove an ancient car have the resources, she assured herself.

Still, she intended to have a chat with Kris just as soon as she got home.

In spite of the disruption of the technician working in the classroom, Joanna made it a point to leave early at the end of the day so there would be time to clear up her questions before football practice.

She parked her car in front of Kris's workshop and walked briskly toward the open doorway.

The heat of summer continued to linger, but the evenings were growing cooler, promising that autumn was on the way, along with a winter season of rain and snow. Glancing up at the building's rotting roof, she knew she was going to have to apply again for a loan at the bank. Surely Wally Petersen wouldn't turn her down now that all the offices were occupied.

She found Kris sitting on one of the two bikes he'd jury-rigged together, both of which were up on stands.

"You'll go faster if the wheels touch the ground," she noted with a smile.

"Oh, hi." He dismounted in a slightly awkward move caused by the closeness of the second bike. "I'm getting things ready for a test ride this weekend. I thought we could try them out on the old railroad grade. That way we won't have to deal with road traffic."

"We?"

"Sure. We'll do it early in the morning, before it gets too hot, and we'll be back in plenty of time for the football game."

"Kris, I haven't agreed to test-drive your bikes. I haven't even been on a bike in years. It doesn't make any sense—"

"That's the whole idea. I want to know if a nonrider can handle the suspension and steering. Balancing may be just a little complicated." He eyed his creation critically. "I may need to make some adjustments."

"Wouldn't it be better if you started your testing with an expert and worked *down* to my skill level?"

"Maybe. But it wouldn't be nearly as much fun."

He flashed that seductive grin of his, the one that made a woman want to agree to anything Kris Slavik asked of her, including a good many things she shouldn't be thinking about.

Joanna resisted—with difficulty. She had another issue on her mind. "We'll talk about it later. Right now I want to know if you've ever heard of a company called Nanosoft Computerware."

"Sure. It's one of the fastest-growing software companies in the country. The stock has doubled in value in the past five years and is still going up."

"Then would you happen to know why that particular company has donated fifty computers to my school?"

"They arrived today? That's terrific." Kris set aside the small wrench he'd been using. "I thought it might take them a week or two to get them out of storage."

"You arranged the contribution?"

"Well, yeah, I guess you could say that." He hesitated. "I kind of know the CEO."

"Kind of?" If Kris had enough clout with the CEO of Nanosoft to get such a large contribution, they must have more than a passing acquaintance.

"He and I went to school together."

That meant the CEO was probably a young man, not unusual in the computer business, she supposed. "Did you work for the company?"

"Yeah. I, ah, was around when the company was founded."

"But you lost your job?"

"Not exactly. I sort of retired."

"Retired? Aren't you a little young to—"

"That's what Chad thought—the CEO. But I didn't see any reason to keep on working."

"No, of course not." That, no doubt, explained the roll of money Kris had carried when he'd first rented the office space. He'd probably taken all of his savings, plus whatever benefit package he might have had, and simply quit his job. Without a family to support, Kris was free to go his own way. Not exactly a decision Joanna would have made, but she had no right to fault him for it. Not everyone carried the responsibility of caring for a child and an aging parent. "Well, it was certainly very thoughtful of you to arrange the contribution from Nanosoft. The children are all very excited."

"That's okay. The computers were just sitting in their warehouse. They aren't state-of-the-art anymore so they won't be missed." Looking a little uncomfortable, he shoved his fingertips into the hip pockets of his jeans. "I also got them to send up some of their prototype games for Tyler. Nothing violent, you understand," he added quickly. "NCC tries to stay clear of those. But I noticed the other night Tyler doesn't have a very big selection—"

"I'm sure he'll be very pleased. Thank you."

"You're welcome." With a flick of his hand, he spun the front tire on one of the bikes. The spokes whizzed around in a silver blur. "So will you help me out by doing the test ride Saturday?"

Joanna had the oddest feeling she'd just been co-opted. How could she say no to a man who had arranged the contribution of several thousand dollars

worth of computers to her school and had been
equally thoughtful when it came to her son? Particularly when, in a tiny spot in her heart, she was un-
duly curious to see how his odd contraption was going to work and painfully eager to help him achieve
success with his crazy invention.

"All right. I'll help you test your high-tech bike,
but only because I'd feel guilty if I didn't."

The victorious look on his face suggested he'd
known all along she would give in to his request.
And, of course, he'd been right.

She walked out of Kris's workshop just as Larry
parked his car in front of his office.

"Hi there, beautiful lady," he called to her.
"Want to help me celebrate?"

"Celebrate?" she echoed.

"Just closed a big deal—megabucks." His smile
was all white teeth and braggadocio. "A girl could
do worse than hooking up with a guy like me. I could
take good care of you, babe. Just say the word."

"No thanks, Larry." She waved him off. "I've
got to get to Tyler's football practice." She'd also
been taking care of herself and her family on her own
for a long time. She didn't need a man for that. Certain other needs, she admitted, she'd repressed for so
long she could hardly give them a name. But Larry,
wealthy or not, wasn't the one who could ease that
particular ache.

As she started to cross the road, she smiled at
Percy and his mother, who were pulling into the
parking lot right behind her. Seriously overweight
and using a cane, Mrs. Carter exited the car with

considerable difficulty. Her son helped her up the two steps and into his office.

Percy was a thoughtful man, Joanna acknowledged. He deserved a full measure of happiness. But there was nothing about him that struck the same powerful chord in her heart that Kris did.

A red-tailed hawk swooped over the top of the pine trees and dove toward the low undergrowth beneath the long string of power lines that crossed through the forested land. Failing to catch his quarry, he rose effortlessly and perched on a power pole to await his next opportunity.

Joanna wished she were as skilled at riding a bike as the hawk was at flying.

"Kris, this isn't working," she complained. She clung to the hand grips with white knuckles, her balance so precarious she could barely pedal the bike.

"We'll get the hang of it in a minute. Keep trying."

They wobbled along the railroad grade, a leftover from the old logging days, for a few more feet. With the tracks and ties removed, the roadway now served as a bike and hiking trail through the woods.

"I thought you said this was going to be romantic." His front tire dipped into a rut; hers tried to follow. She struggled to keep herself upright and in the process made him lose his balance.

He dropped one foot to the ground for balance and strong-armed both the bikes back onto the track. "I may have misjudged a few of the technical requirements for side-by-side riding."

"A few?" she sputtered, choking back a laugh.

"Quite a few," he conceded.

Separated by a couple of metal rods that were only two feet long, the bikes were so close together neither Kris nor Joanna could maneuver effectively, not that the suspension system would have allowed for different destinations, anyway. When they pedaled, their legs brushed, a sensual touching and parting of bare flesh. Their arms did the same with almost every jarring movement. Joanna had never guessed riding a bike could be such an intimate experience. Or quite so much fun.

In response to a dip in the terrain, the trail angled downward. The sudden increase in speed caught Joanna off guard.

She gasped. "Oh, my gosh—" She braked too hard. Her half of the contraption came to a halt while Kris's half skidded around in front of her until they were both aimed across the roadway. The abrupt change in direction unseated her. The bikes slid away, but she wasn't on hers anymore. Instead, after staggering to regain her balance, she came to rest at the side of the trail, falling onto a shady patch of summer-dry grass.

Giggles shook her shoulders and finally ripened into unchecked laughter.

Kris reined the bikes back under control. This wasn't exactly how his testing program was supposed to work, but the sound of Joanna's laughter trilling through the forest was worth every moment he'd spent putting the project together.

He parked the bikes, walked back up the rise and

dropped down beside her. Her face was radiant, her eyes glistening with tears of laughter. He wondered if there had ever been a more beautiful sight in the world and knew he'd never seen anything that even came close.

"I'm s-sorry..." she stammered. A tear escaped her eye and she wiped it away with the back of her hand. "I shouldn't laugh. Not after all your h-hard work...."

"There may be a few glitches that still have to be ironed out. That's not unusual for a prototype." What was unique was how much he enjoyed hearing her laughter and basking in her smile.

"I suppose t-that's true." She placed her hand on his thigh. He didn't think the gesture was meant as a sexual overture, but his body certainly reacted to her light touch and the warmth of her palm. "I hate to be a spoilsport, Kris, but if you were hoping to make a million off this design you might want to rethink your goals."

He feigned a frown. Concern about making another million dollars was at the very bottom of his priorities. "I hate the thought of all that effort being a total waste. Maybe I could sell it to a clown act in a circus."

"Perfect!" she said with a laugh.

He covered her hand with his, and she instantly sobered. Her eyes widened as though she had suddenly realized where her hand had wandered. He held his breath. She didn't move. He didn't want her to. The heat of her hand flowed through his veins right to his groin, and he almost groaned aloud.

The tip of her tongue peeked out and swept across her lips to moisten them. As if an electrical connection had been made, Kris felt the shock low in his body. Tension hummed through him like a live wire sparking out of control.

"Maybe we should be heading back," she said, her voice little more than a whisper in the stillness of the woods.

"No. Not yet." His fingers curled around her hand to prevent her escape. "There's a huge patch of wild blackberries growing up the road a ways. I thought we could pick some." Standing, he tugged her to her feet before she could refuse.

Joanna was tempted to decline his invitation, but picking berries was a better choice than what she really wanted to do—which was to throw herself into his arms and kiss him until she was senseless. That wouldn't take long, she realized. She'd apparently lost most of her good sense as well as her ability to think logically the day Kris Slavik became one of her tenants.

With little effort, he led her down the trail past the bikes, and she fell into step beside him.

If only she hadn't needed the rental money so badly the day he'd handed over a year's worth of rent. It hadn't been enough to cover the entire roof repair job, and with the other two offices vacant, she'd needed it simply to pay the mortgage.

Worry about her finances furrowed her brow. Her visit with the bank manager yesterday hadn't gone as well as she had hoped.

"What's wrong?" Kris asked.

80   ONLY BACHELORS NEED APPLY

"Oh, nothing." She shrugged off his question.

"Then I'll assume you're getting your daily dose of exercise."

She glanced up at him. "What?"

"It takes forty-three muscles to frown and only seventeen to smile. Your frown muscles are definitely getting a workout about now."

"I'm sorry. I didn't mean to turn all glum on you."

"So tell me what's the matter. Did I do something wrong?"

"No, of course not. It's just..." She removed her hand from his, almost instantly missing his reassuring touch. "I visited the bank yesterday. As you may have noticed, the roof on your workshop and the office building is in a sad state of disrepair."

"I did wonder about that, but I'm not exactly an expert on roofs."

"Neither is Wally Petersen, the bank manager. He seems to think the roof will wait until he gets around to approving my loan, which he says will take about thirty days."

They'd reached the berry patch. Kris picked a blackberry and popped it into his mouth. He smiled as he savored the flavor. "But he'll give you the loan then?"

"He's reasonably sure I'll get the approval. Except thirty days may be too late. By then, if we have a heavy rain, the whole thing may well have collapsed. That will double or triple my expense."

"Penny-wise and pound-foolish."

Plucking another berry from the vine, he held it in

front of her mouth. His fingers skimmed her lips as she parted them and accepted his offering. The warm berry juice slid down her throat as another kind of heat spread through her midsection.

Valiantly, she tried to quash the sensation. "I remember when I used to come out here with my friends to pick berries. We'd eat so many we'd practically get sick. Then I'd take the rest home and Mother would bake them up in a pie."

Lifting her chin, he used his thumb to wipe a speck of berry juice from the corner of her mouth. "I don't think my mother has ever made a pie in her life."

"It's not all that difficult." What was hard was to look up into Kris's intensely gray eyes, which had suddenly grown dark, and not want him to kiss her. Evidently he felt the same way.

His head dipped and his lips molded to hers, tasting of sweetness and a strange sort of masculine innocence that was as titillating as it was unexpected. When she gasped with pleasure, he took full advantage of the opportunity, sliding his tongue inside. He was no inexperienced youth, she realized, but a skilled, thoughtful lover.

He teased gently with his tongue and his lips. She responded, knowing she shouldn't, yet unable to stop herself. Never in her life had she been kissed like this, so thoroughly and with such depth of feeling.

Vaguely she was aware of the quiet buzz of insects around the berry bushes and the sound of laughter coming from bikers farther up the trail. But mostly she knew only the feel of Kris's fingertips caressing her neck, the play of his tongue with hers, the throbbing need that was growing ever more insistent low in her body.

Heart beating as though she'd run a mile, she broke the kiss. "I think...I think it's time we went back."

"You're probably right." He seemed as reluctant as she to move, to break the spell of their kiss. "It wouldn't be right to miss our debut as football coaches."

She swallowed hard, forcing down other desires that were so very close to the surface. "The boys would be disappointed."

He ran his knuckles along her cheek. "I'll be disappointed if we don't resume this testing program at a later date."

"I don't think that would be wise." It would be foolhardy beyond belief. She couldn't burden him with the responsibilities she'd chosen to carry.

"I know you think that. And it puzzles me a little. But I suppose I should warn you, I can be very persistent."

Joanna didn't doubt his words for a minute. She simply needed to put some distance between herself and this man who made her want things she knew she couldn't have. It wasn't fair to either of them if she pretended otherwise.

By the time they got back home, Tyler was already pacing in front of Kris's workshop, waiting for them.

"Man, I thought you guys had forgotten about the game."

"Not a chance." Kris unstrapped the dual bikes from the flatbed trailer he'd rented. "We just had some problems with the first run of the prototype. It'll go better after I make a few adjustments.''

Tyler helped him lift the bikes down and wheel them toward the garage. "I wish my buddy, Pete, could ride something like this.''

"The blind boy?'' Kris asked.

"Yeah. His older brother is heavy into mountain-bike racing, but the officials won't let Pete enter with him on a tandem.''

"Why not? It doesn't seem to me that would hurt the other competitors.''

"I dunno. Something about the rules saying all the entrants have to pedal under their own power. Pete's plenty strong enough. He just can't see where he's going.''

Rubbing his hand along the back of his neck, Kris studied the dual contraption he'd created.

"Oh-oh,'' Joanna teased. "The master is thinking about another million-dollar invention.''

He slanted her an amused look. "Nope. But I might try to come up with something that would let a blind kid participate in a bike race. That ought to be worth a whole lot more than money.''

Joanna agreed, and her heart swelled with new admiration for this man who had such a powerful effect on her. Why on earth couldn't she think of him as a ne'er-do-well, an unemployed bum who tinkered his life away without accepting any responsibility? Her life would be a whole lot easier if she did.

Chapter Six

"Did you know Americans eat about a billion hot dogs every year?"

Joanna's head snapped up. After football practice and a quick dinner, she'd come to the school carnival where she was helping out at the PTA hot dog booth. Now, Kris's gray eyes snared her as she was in the act of putting a hot dog on a bun. His hair was slightly damp and curled at his nape as if he'd just come from his shower; his T-shirt tugged across broad shoulders, tapering in at a narrow waist. The man would be a serious distraction for a nun, and Joanna's long celibacy matched that of a disciple in the strictest religious order.

She'd never intended to live that way but knew she had no other choice. Emotionally, she couldn't handle an uncommitted relationship, not after her experience with Tyler's father. Nor could she allow herself to be a poor role model for her son. And as a girl who lived in a house festooned with whirligigs, a girl whose parents and grandparents acted bizarrely, she had never found anyone remotely interested in pursuing a long-term commitment. Not that she would have asked anyone else to accept the weight of baggage she carried on her shoulders.

With an effort of will, she swallowed back a lifetime of regret.

"Are there any bits of trivia that aren't stored in that brain of yours?" she asked.

"Probably not many. I hung out in the library a lot when I was a kid, and I have a photographic memory." He said it easily, as if everyone could read a page and then repeat all the information in precise detail years later.

"So you blame it all on a misspent youth?" she teased. She passed the hot dog to a young customer. Maureen, who was staffing the booth with Joanna, ordered hot dogs for a family of five and poured their cold drinks. The mother of six children herself, one of whom was currently in Joanna's fourth-grade class, Maureen had made a career of volunteering for PTA projects. Bless her heart.

"It's occurred to me lately that I may have missed out on some things," Kris said.

"Like what?"

The corners of his lips quirked.

"I shouldn't have asked that," she said hastily, feeling a blush heat her cheeks, suspecting he was thinking about a whole slew of forbidden topics just as she had been. She was missing out on a lot, too—

the big family she'd always dreamed about and the love of one special man.

She passed the hot dogs and buns to Maureen.

"It's all right," Kris said. "I'm in the process of making up for lost time." He leaned his elbow on the plastic top of the hot-dog cooker, that tempting smile still playing at the corners of his lips. "For instance, I'm about to lure you away to ride the Ferris wheel with me."

She glanced across the school yard to the gaily lighted rides, the source of tinny music and childish laughter. "Sorry, I can't. I promised—"

"Oh, go ahead," Maureen insisted. "Go with the man. The big rush is over and we've only got a half hour left on our shift. Have a good time. I'll manage."

"I don't want to leave you in the lurch," Joanna protested.

"Honey!" Maureen hooted. "If I had a good-lookin' hunk like that askin' me to go anywhere with him, I'd be outta here so fast it'd make your head spin. A gal can cook hot dogs any ol' time. Now him—" she nodded toward Kris "—I'd land that fella and hog-tie him before he had a chance to get away, if I was you."

"Thank you, ma'am." Kris dipped his head.

"But—" Joanna sputtered.

"Go on, you two." Maureen made a shooing motion with her hands. "And have fun. Teachers shouldn't have to work the carnival, anyways. They do enough by putting up with our kids all week long."

Defeated by Maureen's insistence—and Kris's persistence—Joanna untied her apron. It seemed that the entire town of Twain Harte was set on match-making.

The moment she stepped out from behind the booth, Kris slipped his arm around her waist. If he got his way, he was the one who was going to do the hog-tying. Ever since that morning when he'd kissed her, he'd been looking for an excuse to do it again. In fact, he would like to make a habit of kissing Joanna Greer.

Tonight she was wearing a dark-colored sweater made of a clingy fabric he ached to touch. Over the top, but doing little to disguise her feminine figure, she wore a long, sleeveless vest in a lighter shade. A cameo charm hung from a chain around her neck and nestled in that fascinating spot right between her breasts. Her sculpted earrings dangled and flashed, catching the light and throwing it back at him.

Kris suddenly wished he'd paid more attention to the locker-room conversations he'd heard among the guys who were studs. As a student, he'd been far more interested in computing exotic mathematical formulas than in pursuing women. He should have at least taken some notes for future reference.

Maybe he'd call Chad in the next couple of days for advice. His business partner had never had trouble with women, except for the problem of escaping their pursuit.

When they reached the Ferris wheel, Kris handed two tickets to the operator, then helped Joanna into the seat and joined her, snapping the safety bar in place. He casually draped his arm around the back of the chair, letting his fingers rest on the curve of her shoulder. Lord, he felt like an inept adolescent on the make. He really needed to get some help.

"Pretty neat, eh?" he said as the wheel rocked them back. It wasn't the most scintillating conversation opener a guy could think of, but the best Kris could manage when the faint trace of Joanna's floral perfume was about to drive him crazy.

"It's not exactly the biggest Ferris wheel in the world."

"Maybe not, but it's the first one I've ever ridden."

She raised her eyebrows in surprise. "How on earth did you reach the age of..." Her brows tightened into a frown. "How old are you?"

"Thirty-one."

"Then how have you managed this long without ever riding a Ferris wheel?"

"I've never ridden on a roller coaster, either. Deprived childhood, I suppose."

An unwelcome tug of sympathy pulled at her heart. "Did you grow up poor?"

"Nope. Strictly middle class. Both my parents are full professors at UC Berkeley. Dad's in astrophysics and Mother specializes in microbiology. They both emigrated from Russia with their parents when they were quite young, and they spent most of their early years in this country nearly penniless. Excelling at academics was important to them. Going to amusement parks was pretty far down on their priority list when we were growing up."

"There's more than one of you? I mean, you have siblings?"

"A sister. Rochelle. She's an assistant professor at MIT. Robotics is her specialty."

"Good grief! Does that mean you're the black sheep of the family?"

He chuckled. "Yeah, I guess I am. They opposed my going into business instead of entering academia."

"I see. Does that mean your current unemployment is just another way to rebel against your parents?"

He remained thoughtfully quiet as the Ferris wheel rocked them over the top of its arc and swung them down toward the crowded school yard again.

"Maybe that's what I'm doing, but not consciously. I never had a chance to be a kid, Joanna. I never played sports like Tyler does. When other guys were inviting girls to the prom, I was holed up in a lab or lashed to my computer. At the time, that's what I wanted to do."

"And now you want to sow some wild oats?"

"Now I want to see how the other half lives. I want to be a normal guy. I want to invite you to the prom—and anywhere else you'll go with me."

"It's a little late for both of us to be talking about a prom date. That's for adolescents with dreams. Not for adults with responsibilities."

He toyed with her hair, shifting the strands at her nape lightly like a warm current of air. Little ripples of warmth slid down her spine. "Did someone take your dream away?"

"Yes." Her throat tightened at the admission. It wasn't just the man who'd abandoned her when she'd become pregnant who'd stolen her dreams, as Kris probably suspected. It was her grandmother, who used to put up Christmas lights in July and play a trombone—badly—during a full moon, and who'd collected every bit of string that had ever come her way. It was Joanna's mother, who had purple and apricot and chartreuse days, and her father, who had loved the sound of whirling wings on his roof. And so, Lord help her, did Joanna.

Tyler's father had been less than enthralled by her family's eccentricities, as were his parents. Appalled came closer to the truth.

The Ferris wheel stopped, suspending them at the apex. The chair creaked as it rocked back and forth. Above them, the night sky was filled with stars, the Milky Way a faint silver arc across the darkness. Below, the crowds had begun to disperse. Lights blinked off as booths closed down and volunteers began to clean up the debris from the carnival.

Lifting his hand, Kris palmed her cheek. He turned her face toward him.

"Maybe we can find a new dream together," he said, his voice husky. "One that works for both of us."

Her heart thudded against her ribs. "I don't think so, Kris." No man needed the embarrassment her family would bring him, or the financial and emotional burdens. It simply wasn't fair.

Joanna pulled the trash can from under the sink late the following afternoon. In the process, a puddle of water spilled out of the cupboard and onto the floor.

She sighed. That did not bode well for Kris's reputation as a skilled plumber. Squatting down, she peered under the sink, but knew there was little she could do. She would either have to ask Kris for his help again or wait until next week. Clearly she needed to enroll in a home-handyman class at the local community college so she could learn to make these minor repairs herself. A woman shouldn't be dependent upon a man, she told herself. Not for fixing things around the house. Or for giving her the love she so desperately wanted.

She looked up as her mother came in from the garden through the back door, her work gloves in one hand and her clippers in the other. Her straw hat was slightly askew, and she had a streak of dirt on her cheek.

"Gracious, but my roses are doing so well this year it almost looks like spring. Your father did love my roses so." She stopped in the middle of the room and gazed without apparent surprise at the floor in front of the sink. "There's a puddle of water, dear. Did you notice?"

"Yes, Mother, I noticed. I just haven't quite decided what to do about it yet."

"You'll have to ask Kris to fix the disposal again, of course." She put her gloves and clippers on the kitchen table. "He's such a nice young man. Maybe we should ask him to stay for dinner after—"

"Mother, the leak isn't very bad. I can put a pail

under it and call a plumber tomorrow. It can't cost all that much—"

"Your father used to particularly enjoy oven-baked chicken and biscuits with my homemade jam. Yes, I think that's what he'd like tonight." Taking off her hat, she fussed with her hair. "When he gets home from work, I'll ask him to run out to the store. He won't mind. He's so good about that sort of thing."

"Mother? Are you talking about Dad or Kris?"

"Why, I..." A confused look came into her mother's eyes and her hand trembled as she smoothed curls still tinged with purple. "Don't bother about me, dear. I know I ramble on. But I do think you'd be wise to ask Kris for help. I wouldn't want that leak to get worse and overflow during the night. Your father worked so hard laying this flooring, he'd be very disturbed if it was damaged, don't you think? We'd never be able to get all those sample swatches from the store arranged so cleverly again. It was such an economy."

"Yes, Mother, of course." The press of tears stung at the back of Joanna's eyes. Her father had been gone for two years, yet her mother continued to speak of him in the present tense. And the floor she raved about was decidedly unique in appearance, each square a different pattern or color. "I'll see if Kris is there now. Will you be all right alone for a few minutes?"

"I'll be fine. I'll just...I do believe I'll take a little nap. I feel so tired." Distractedly, Agnes picked up her gloves, clippers and hat and walked toward her bedroom. She mumbled to herself as if trying to remember what had made her feel so weary.

Joanna thought her heart would break. Her parents had had such a wonderful, loving relationship, and now her mother was left clinging to memories that, in her confused state of mind, seemed more real to her than the present.

But there was no help for it. Joanna had to ask Kris to fix the leak under the sink. She couldn't risk upsetting her mother further. It simply wasn't fair.

Long, black extension cords snaked across the ground from Kris's office to his workshop. He'd set up additional overhead lighting, a new workbench that was strewn with electrical wires in a rainbow of colors, and he'd added a computer station equipped with a modem.

Dumbfounded, Joanna didn't know what to make of the array of electronic devices and wondered why the dual bikes had been disassembled. They were propped separately against the far wall, with wires connecting the frames to something that looked like a tiny satellite dish and to the computer.

"What are you up to?" she asked.

He glanced up from the computer keyboard. His hair was rumpled and he looked as though he hadn't shaved all day. Sandy-blond whiskers roughened his cheeks, making his jaw appear more firm, square and masculine—even more appealing.

"It's my new invention. I've been working on it since last night. I'm using smart-bomb technology."

"You're making a bomb?" Vaguely, she wondered if next time she should put something in her lease agreement to prevent lunatic inventors from blowing up her building—a building that carried a very large mortgage, needed a new roof and didn't have half enough insurance. "Who are you planning to attack? The opposing football team?" she teased.

"Nope. But Tyler's going to be the target. He's already agreed."

"Doesn't a minor being a target require parental permission? I don't think I approve."

Grinning, Kris swiveled around on his chair. "It's for Pete."

"Pete Ashford?"

"Yeah. See, I'm planning to put a target on one bike—that's the one Tyler's going to ride. Then the other bike—Peter's—is going to lock onto that target electronically. Pete will hear a tone in these earphones." Kris held up a big black pair that had been sitting on top of the computer. "That'll tell him to go right or left. On another frequency there'll be a beeping sound that'll let him know how close he is to the target. The faster the beeps go, the closer he is. The object is to maintain a steady distance between Tyler's bike and Pete's on the same track."

Slack jawed, Joanna tried to absorb what he had just explained. "You're amazing."

"Pretty neat, huh?" He motioned for her to come closer. "Here, put on these earphones and I'll show you what I mean."

She did as instructed, adjusting the earmuffs so they fit snugly. In a one-finger dance across the keyboard, Kris gave instructions to the computer. She heard a steady hum in both ears.

"Listen to what happens when you drift off to the right," he said as he tapped the keyboard again.

Her eyes widened as the hum grew progressively louder in her left ear. "That's wonderful, but how is Pete going to—"

"When the hum increases in his left ear, he'll steer left. Simple."

She nodded. It all sounded so easy when Kris explained it.

"Now listen to the distance beep. It's like a sonar bleep."

It was, she agreed. Even she had watched enough submarine movies to recognize it. "Just one question. Who's going to run along behind these bikes and carry the computer?"

He burst out laughing and turned back to his keyboard. "Guess I'll have to think of something, won't I?"

A movement at the corner of Joanna's eye caught her attention.

She glanced that direction as Larry Smythe stormed into the workshop. "What the hell is going on out here?"

Apparently Kris was so intent on his demonstration, he didn't immediately react to the angry accusation, and his fingers continued to issue commands to the computer.

Joanna slipped off the earphones. "Kris is working on a new project."

"What he's doing is messing up my computer!"

Larry bellowed. "I've had two power surges in the last half hour that have dumped all my data, and now I've lost my link to the multiple-listing board."

"No reason why that should happen," Kris muttered.

"Well, it did."

With obvious reluctance, Kris tore his concentration away from the keyboard and looked up. "I'll check out the circuits. I shouldn't be pulling that much power."

Eager to smooth over Larry's ruffled feathers, Joanna said, "Kris's new invention is going to let a young blind boy ride in a mountain-bike race." Assuming Peter could comprehend the odd beeps and hums he'd hear in the earphones. "It's a very exciting idea." If not a hundred percent practical, and barely understandable as far as she was concerned, it certainly was sweet of Kris to make the effort. Though she had her doubts, she hoped the concept worked.

"That's nonsense," Larry groused. "Why would a blind kid want to ride a bike? He'd probably break his neck. Instead, he ought to be at home studying braille or something."

Joanna bristled—on behalf of Peter, and especially Kris, who was trying to do something quite wonderful. She planted her fist on her hip.

"Now listen here, Mr. Smythe. Just because a child is blind doesn't mean he has to be pigeonholed his whole life. With enough help from people like Kris and all of his technical expertise, Peter will be able to do any darn thing he wants. And I won't have you criticizing Kris when you're—you're..." She fumed. There wasn't a ladylike word to describe how she felt about an arrogant man like Larry.

His chest puffed out as if he'd inhaled a balloonful of hot air. "I didn't realize, Ms. Greer—"

Kris stood and slid his arm around Joanna's rigid shoulders in a reassuring embrace that was both calming and achingly arousing. "Like I said, Larry, I'll check the wiring. But I'd suggest you hit the Save command more often if you don't want to lose your data, and buy a surge protector. The power in this community is a little erratic."

Larry glared daggers at them. "I'll do that, Slavik." Whirling, he stomped out of the workshop toward his office.

Joanna exhaled the breath she'd been holding and slumped against Kris. She'd probably just lost a tenant. For the moment, she didn't give a damn. Larry was rude and arrogant. If she didn't need his monthly rent money, she'd throw him out on his ear herself.

"Thanks for defending me," Kris said.

She raised her gaze to meet his. "Why wouldn't I? You're doing something wonderful for Peter. If it works, if he can actually participate in a bike race, he'll be in seventh heaven."

"And if it doesn't work?"

"You'll still have tried. Nobody can ask more of you than that."

"A lot of people would simply dismiss me as an intellectual with his head in the clouds."

"I don't." She couldn't dismiss him at all. That certainly was impossible when she was standing in the circle of his arm, his compellingly masculine scent surrounding her, his incredible intelligence and creative mind holding her in awe. Slowly, realization dawned and she was struck by the knowledge of how truly brilliant he was. "You're a genius." Her words were a breathless statement of fact.

"I'm a man, Joanna. A guy who'd someday like to have a wife and family of his own, maybe some kids to play touch football with or teach how to use a computer. I'm just a man."

His lips brushed hers in a heated caress, as if to emphasize his point.

She leaned into his kiss. Dimly she realized she shouldn't be doing this. They had no future together. To encourage him was wrong. However intelligent he was—or perhaps because of his brilliance—he wouldn't want to be saddled with her bizarre inheritance.

Sliding her palms up his chest, across the soft fabric of his T-shirt, she struggled against the urge to link her hands behind his neck, sink her fingers into his long hair and pull him more tightly to her. But that would be foolhardy.

For the past ten years she'd tried to remain resolute in accepting the cards fate had dealt her. Now was not the time to weaken.

"I've got to go," she whispered against his lips.

"Sure. I understand."

He released her slowly, and she ached with the futile desire that he never would do so.

She was all the way back home before she realized

she hadn't even mentioned her plumbing problem to Kris.

Getting down on her knees in front of the kitchen sink, she studied the connections for the garbage disposal, then tested them with her fingertips. They looked and felt as dry as a bone. There wasn't a leak and never had been.

Heaving a sigh, she concluded she'd been conned by her mother once again. In spite of Agnes's frequent forgetfulness, she was as sly as a fox when it came to matchmaking.

Chapter Seven

Groggy from a forty-eight-hour stint at his computer, Kris hefted the oxygen bottle and settled it on his back. The fire jacket was bulky, restricting his movements, and the hat slipped a little too low on his forehead.

"You expect us to put out a fire wearing all of this gear?" he asked, only partly in jest. "I can hardly move."

"I expect that gear to save your hide from getting scorched, young man. That's what it's for." Joshua Bigelow, the volunteer fire department's chief and a retired big-city fireman, adjusted the straps on Kris's shoulders, then gave him a one-of-the-boys slap on the back. "Go get yourself some hose, son."

Kris joined the rest of the volunteers as they strung the hose from the fire truck across the empty school parking lot. Floodlights at the corners of the building illuminated the grounds, cutting through the night-time shadows.

The dozen volunteers-in-training that evening were all from the community—a couple of utility workers, the owner of a Mexican restaurant, a building contractor or two, the son of the bank president, and a guy who cut firewood for a living. Kris liked them all. He liked taking part in their easy camaraderie. He'd rarely enjoyed man-to-man bonding such as this. Up till now he'd been far too focused on developing exotic computer programs.

Women hadn't been an issue before, either. Now, knowing Joanna, he again wished he'd paid more attention. He could use a whole hell of a lot more self-confidence when it came to her. She was definitely one test he'd hate to fail.

In pairs, Kris and the other volunteer firemen lifted the hoses and marched to attack a mock fire.

"Come on, Slavik," the trainer shouted. "Nestle up and hang on to that hose like your life depends on it. You lose contact with your buddy in a smoky building and you may not get out of there."

"Right." Kris had a fleeting thought that there ought to be a better, safer way to get in and out of a burning building even if it was smoky. Radar could see through—

The hose came alive with water, a powerful snake that tried to wrench itself free of Kris's grasp. He hung on. Barely. And he and his buddy moved forward while Bigelow shouted, "Teamwork, men! Lick that devil fire!"

Behind his visor, Kris grinned. His boyhood dream had come true. He was a real-life fireman.

Joanna glanced at Kris's workshop as she drove by after school.

Except for football practices, she hadn't seen him at all that week. Even at practice he'd seemed as distracted as her mother sometimes was, leaving early without even telling the boys—or her—goodbye

Whenever she'd chanced a look at his workshop, the big door was open and the lights were on, including once in the wee hours of the morning when her restless dreams woke her and she peered out her window with longing.

She wondered if he was eating right; she worried that he might electrocute himself. She chided herself for the twinge of resentment that he was more engrossed in "The Invention" than he was in her. She cursed herself for her volatile emotions, which had never before been so out of control.

Until Kris moved into her rental property, she'd felt her life was very nearly what she wanted. Very nearly.

She might not have a husband, but she did have Tyler to love. As trying as her mother might sometimes be, Joanna always felt wrapped in her love. Teaching was a fulfilling if wearing occupation, and she wouldn't ever want that to change.

But Kris had unsettled her comfortable cocoon. He made her want things she'd been told she couldn't have. That was terribly unfair and disturbing because she didn't know how to deal with her feelings, emotions that seemed to tumble all over themselves like rain clouds buffeting a mountain peak.

She'd parked in her garage and had barely gotten into the house when Tyler arrived.

"Hey, Mom! Kris is ready for us to test the bikes. Pete's on his way over." He dashed through the living room and was back an instant later, his bicycle helmet in his hand. "We're using the parking lot in front of Kris's place. You wanna come watch? It's gonna be totally awesome."

"Yes, I guess—"

"I'll see you there." He blasted out the door as if he was rocket propelled.

She stood staring at the closed door a moment. Evidently Tyler had had more communication with Kris recently than she had.

Not wanting to seem overly eager to see her tenant, Joanna took her time changing out of her work clothes and into jeans and a sweatshirt. She combed her hair, then gave up pretending. She didn't want to miss the unveiling of Kris's creation. And she wanted very much to see him.

She hurried outside and up the street.

He looked tired. Lines of sleeplessness etched his face and he looked as if he could use a shower and a good meal. The man needed a caretaker, she realized.

Or a wife.

He smiled wearily as she walked across the parking lot toward him, and a band of regret tightened around her chest. He deserved more than she could give him.

"Hi," she said. "This is the big day, huh?"

"I hope so." His gaze lingered on her momentarily—almost hungrily—before returning to his two young protegés. "All right, guys. This is what I want you to do."

Following Kris's instructions, the boys mounted their respective bikes, with Tyler lining up a few feet in front of Pete. Kris fussed with the earphones and adjusted the devices stuck on the front and back of the two bikes. Pete, who was as darkly complected as Tyler was fair, looked anxious. Tyler was grinning confidently.

"Where did you get all these electronic bits and pieces?" she asked.

"I've got a friend with a pretty big warehouse."

"The same one who used to have a lot of spare computers?"

"He still does. They go obsolete pretty fast."

Joanna followed Kris around to the opposite side of the bikes. "Isn't all this smart-bomb stuff classified? I'd hate for my son to be arrested as a spy or something."

Crouching down, he attached two leads to a miniature satellite dish, checked the reading on his meter, then said, "Most of it's already been written up in *Aviation Week*. Pretty hard to keep a secret in this country."

Apparently satisfied with the results of his tinkering, he stood and placed his hand on Pete's shoulder.

"We'll do a straight run first—to the end of the

parking lot. It's only about a hundred and fifty feet, Pete, so don't overtake Tyler when he gets to the end. You hear those beeps coming at you fast, you put on your brakes.''

"Yes, sir.''

''You're sure you've ridden a bike before?''

''Lots of times,'' Pete said. ''With my brother.''

''Okay. Get ready.'' The boys steadied themselves on their bikes. ''On your mark, get set, go!''

Tyler took off, pedaling hard. Pete was right behind him, amazingly well balanced for a boy who could see little more than shadows. Joanna thought he was incredibly brave to ride into unknown territory.

She held her breath. Seconds passed.

The boys reached the end of the course far sooner than she expected. Tyler pulled up before he reached the split-rail fence at the far side of the property. Pete didn't react quickly enough. His bike slammed into the back of Tyler's; he toppled head over heels and fell against the fence.

Praying that neither boy had sustained major injuries, Joanna broke into a run. Kris was already two steps ahead of her.

They reached the boys only to discover them whooping and hollering in joy.

''I did it, Kris!'' Pete shouted, hugging his buddy. He pumped a victorious fist in the air. ''All on my own! I rode a bike by myself! Did you see me, Ms. Greer?''

''I certainly did. You were wonderful. Both of you.'' She wanted to hug the boys, and Kris, too.

She met his gaze over the jumble of bikes and youngsters. She'd never felt so proud of anything in her life. She saw it in his eyes, as well—his pride in accomplishment, his love for the boys. And something low and achy responded deep in her soul.

She reached out her hand and he took it, squeezing her fingers tightly. "There appears to be a kamikaze element at work here I hadn't previously identified," he said.

Her lips twitched in a near smile. "I think it's something about being ten years old. They're invincible." In her eyes, so was Kris—a knight in shining armor who was ready and able to slay the most dangerous of dragons.

Pete scrambled to his feet. "So, can we do it again?"

"Yeah, I'm ready," Tyler echoed.

"Okay, but next time go a little slower," Kris suggested. "We're going to try a few S-turns. Nothing fancy, Tyler. I want to see if Pete can track you."

"All right!" they chorused, both boys hauling their bikes upright again.

"Wait a minute. I've got to check out the electronic gear. It's not exactly designed for a high-speed crash. We've gotta take the bikes back to the lab." Kris examined the front of Pete's bike. "There's something else you both ought to know."

"What's that?"

"I checked the racing schedule. The next race you two would be eligible to enter is this Saturday."

"We'll be ready," Tyler said.

"Darn right," Pete agreed. "We can skip school to practice, if you want."

"Oh, no, you can't," Joanna admonished.

With a slight lift of his lips, Kris ignored Pete's comment. "The race time conflicts with your football game against the Vikings, Tyler. It's a big game, son. You're going to have to choose."

Joanna saw the indecision in her son's eyes. He was the team's quarterback. Football was his life.

"When is the next race after that?" the boy asked.

"Locally, not until next spring," Kris told him. "It's possible I could find something on the schedule down south, maybe around Palm Springs. The season's pretty well over here."

Pete's shoulders slumped. "It's okay, Tyler. We can wait till next year. The game's important—"

"No." Tyler clamped his hand over his friend's shoulder. "We're gonna do this. No way am I gonna let you sit on your butt while I'm gettin' creamed by those Vikings. They're awesome. Besides, Brandis has been going bananas wanting to play quarterback. He'd be okay."

Tyler glanced at his mother and she simply nodded, unable to express her feelings at the moment. She was so proud of her son she thought she might burst. He was making a huge sacrifice. Somehow Kris, through his brilliance, had made this possible. He'd touched the lives of two boys. Win or lose, neither of them would forget the experience.

The boys were wheeling the bikes back to Kris's workshop when a car pulled into the lot. To Joanna's surprise, it was Isabel Currant and her son, Cody.

Isabel rolled down the window on the driver's side. "Hello, Ms. Greer. I was just coming to see you."

"Oh? What can I do for you?"

"Well, my husband and I..." She glanced at her son in the passenger seat, a child who looked more sullen than eager to be back. "We're going to try to make a go of it again. And I thought—that is, Paul wants to continue coaching Cody's team. I know you and Mr. Slavik have been filling in, but I wondered if—"

"Of course, Mrs. Currant. You go ahead. We were simply helping out since there was no one else." At least one problem would be solved by the reappearance of the Currant family. Both Joanna and Kris would be able to attend the bike race the coming weekend. Like her son, she thought it a far more important event than a weekly football game. She doubted Paul Currant would agree.

Hopefully the returning coach wouldn't take out his displeasure on Tyler.

For the rest of the week, the boys spent all of their spare time practicing on their bikes. Once they mastered simple turns on the level parking lot, Kris took them to the railroad grade for more realistic training.

Tyler came home with a couple of skinned knees and a scraped elbow. Joanna didn't even want to think about all of Peter's bruises, since he was the one who took most of the falls. She'd even talked with his parents. In their usual fashion, they'd decided that if Peter wanted to ride in a race, he should.

Though Joanna was sure they gritted their teeth and held their breath at some of the feats Peter attempted, they were determined to let him be as normal as possible. A few bruises and skinned knees were a small price to pay for the chance to let him grow into a whole man.

And, as Joanna observed the events unfolding, she was sure she'd never known two boys—no, make that *three men*—who were more determined to succeed.

She had all the symptoms of a pending anxiety attack by the time race day arrived. Her stomach was churning, her palms were sweaty and she had trouble drawing a deep breath.

Near the starting line, vendors of bicycle accessories displayed their wares beneath colorful awnings. The sun shone brightly on the crowd that milled around between various heats, bikers renewing friendships and offering encouragement to other participants, both novice and expert.

Peter's parents mixed with the crowd. They looked relaxed, but Joanna suspected that was a masquerade. Surely they were as anxious as she was.

"I only hope the boys don't get hurt," Joanna told Kris as they waited for the starting signal.

Sensing her nervousness, he took her nd. "They're tough kids. They'll do fine." He'd ne about all he could, given the short time he'd had for the design-and-development phase of the project. The electronics were still heavier than he'd like, creating some balance problems, and a bit too fragile. Something as simple as dust or a flying rock could cause the whole system to break down. Or another biker could come between Tyler and Pete, distorting the tracking signal and sending Pete off the trail.

Shoot, he was as anxious as Joanna.

She squeezed his hand. "In case I've forgotten to mention it, I think it's pretty terrific what you've done for Pete."

Kris wanted to bask in her praise but feared it was a little premature. "You might not think so if one or both of those kids break their respective necks."

"You just told me they'll be fine."

The riders in the novice heat jostled for position near the front of the pack, and the starter readied his gun.

"I don't know about you," Kris said, "but I think I may throw up."

"Me, too." Joanna laughed nervously. "We're quite a pair, aren't we?"

Smiling, he glanced down at her. The sun streaked her hair with highlights, catching the curls like diamonds dancing across the swells in San Francisco Bay. He hoped this project didn't end in disaster. If nothing else, he wanted this woman to be impressed with his engineering skills. More importantly, he wanted her to be impressed with him.

The gun sounded. Joanna flinched.

The mob of bikers pedaled up the hill, the steepest part of the trail. Tyler and Pete stayed near the back of the pack. Joanna thought that was fine. Less chance of an accident that way.

"They go twice around the course," Kris told her

as the last of the bikes vanished out of sight over the rise.

Minutes ticked by. Some of the onlookers wandered off. The wait seemed interminable.

"How much longer?" she asked. Her breathing was labored; her nerves tightened her throat.

"A couple of minutes."

She squeezed Kris's hand so hard she knew it must hurt. But she didn't want to let him go. Not ever. And certainly not now.

It was only a race, she told herself. The boys weren't expecting to win. They simply wanted to finish.

A cheer from the front of the crowd announced the lead bikers coming into sight. Two boys, both older than Tyler and Pete, came barreling down the hill side by side, slid into the turn and shot up the hill again, to begin the second lap of the race. More entrants appeared, the pack of riders strung out now along the course.

Joanna strained to spot her son and his friend.

Then suddenly there they were, riding more cautiously than the leaders but still in the race.

"Come on, Tyler!" she cheered. "Way to go, Peter!"

The rest of the crowd, aware of Peter's disability, added their enthusiastic applause and shouts of encouragement.

Intent on their race, neither boy visibly responded to the vocal support. But Joanna knew they must be thrilled by what they had already accomplished.

It wasn't long until the winning biker crossed the

finish line, dust flying beneath his wheels. He was quickly followed by the bulk of the entrants.

A couple of stragglers showed up, their legs covered in mud, their goggles dusty and their shirts sweaty. But there was still no sign of Tyler and Peter.

As though of one mind, the crowd seemed to hold its collective breath waiting for the two final entrants. Kris shoved his way toward the finish line; Joanna followed in his wake. She'd lost track of where Peter's parents were in the crowd but knew they must be as worried as she was.

Recognizing a boy she'd once had in her class, Joanna asked, "What about Peter and Tyler? Did you see them?"

The youngster lifted his helmet off and shoved his goggles to the top of his head. "Peter went down on the backside of the course."

"Was he hurt?"

"I don't think so. Least ways, not bad. Tyler waved us on past. I think maybe they blew a tire."

Kris's arm slid around her shoulder. "Tyler's got a repair kit. They'll make it. You'll see. Even if they have to carry the bikes."

Joanna wished she shared Kris's confidence.

A cheer went up from the crowd.

At the top of the hill, two riders appeared. Joanna's weepy smile broadened as she recognized her son in the lead. Pete's front tire was practically touching Tyler's back wheel and both boys were pedaling hard, giving it their all even if they were in last place. They looked as if they'd been rolling in the mud and so did their bikes.

To Joanna's surprise, at the last second before crossing the line, Tyler shouted, ''Go for it, Pete! Straight ahead!'' He pulled up, out of the way, letting Pete finish before him.

The crowd roared in approval.

Love and pride burst within Joanna's chest. She stood, tears rolling down her cheeks, as Pete's father went running after his son to stop him before he crashed and seriously damaged himself. Meanwhile, with the arrogance of youth, Tyler waved to his adoring audience.

Joanna turned to Kris. ''Thank you,'' she whispered.

''Don't thank me. Your son's one terrific youngster.''

''You're the one who gave him the chance to be all that he could be.''

Standing on tiptoe, she kissed Kris. She thought she was kissing him as another way to say thank-you. Or perhaps as a part of the celebration that was going on around them. But it quickly became more than that.

Crowd noises ebbed and flowed around her, but she was only vaguely aware of them. She was, in that instant, gloriously female and Kris was all-male. Strong. Intelligent. Sexy. He tasted of something rare and wonderful, a mix of both power and sensitivity. She drank in his flavor.

A tormented moan rose in her throat as she realized she loved Kristopher Slavik. Completely and thoroughly. No longer could she deny the truth of that, even to herself. Though the revelation changed nothing.

She could not, dared not, act on that love, more for his sake than her own. He wanted a family, and what she had to offer was more burden than blessing. Both Tyler's father and his parents had made that abundantly clear. Kris deserved better.

Eventually Joanna made her way to her son and gave him a well-deserved hug. He smelled of sweat and mud, but his smile was about as broad as the whole Sierra range.

"You did good, tiger," she said. "You, too, Pete. Great race."

"We came in last," Tyler stated.

"You never gave up and you got to the finish line. You're both very special young men."

A blush stained Tyler's cheeks. "Ah, gee, Mom..."

Chapter Eight

Through the rest of the weekend Joanna held the knowledge of her love for Kris in her heart. She couldn't let it go. Not yet. It was too precious a commodity for her not to savor the feeling for a little while. Then she would have to put it behind her, as she had set aside other dreams.

She rounded the last curve in the road on her way home from school on Monday and saw smoke rising above her rental property, a fire truck parked out front. Panic snared her breath, blocking a scream of fear and desperation in her lungs.

She burst out of her car almost before it had come to a full stop and ran toward the fire truck.

"Easy, Ms. Greer," Chief Bigelow drawled. He caught her by the arm before she could do something really stupid, like run right into Percy's office, which appeared to be the source of the cloud of white smoke. "My boys have got things under control."

"Was anyone hurt? Is Percy all right?"

"My newest recruit, that young Slavik fellow, got Percy's mother out of the building safe and sound. Other than the two of them, nobody else was around. They're both fine."

Joanna heaved a sigh of relief, then coughed as remnants of acrid smoke caught in her lungs. "What started the fire?"

"We'll have to check on that after things cool off. But based on what I've seen, I'd guess the wiring in this old building was at fault. Probably an overload."

"Overload," she muttered. Too much exotic electronic equipment, she supposed. "Where is Mrs. Carter now?"

"The paramedics are looking her over. A little oxygen and she ought to be fit again. It was mighty smoky in there for a while."

"And Kris?"

"He's with her. Good man even if he is into heroics. Quick thinker. Called 9-1-1 before he risked his own neck." Bigelow glanced up at one of his firemen, who was standing on the roof, and waved him off. "We did have to chop a hole in your roof to let the heat out. You'll be wanting to have that repaired soon."

"Yes, of course." She thanked the chief and his crew for their rapid response to the fire. She supposed it was better to have a hole burned in her roof before repairs had been made rather than after. Neither choice, however, seemed particularly attractive.

She went in search of Kris and Mrs. Carter, finding them just as Percy pulled up in his car.

"Percival!" his mother wailed, shoving the oxygen mask away from her face. "Where have you been?"

"I'm here now, Mummy dear. What happened?"

"I could have died, that's what happened. You left me all alone," she sobbed.

"I'm back now, dearest." As Percy made a valiant effort to console his mother, Joanna went to Kris.

"Are you all right?" she asked.

"I'm fine. So was Mrs. Carter until her son showed up. She's just a little shaken, is all. She's not too agile on her feet and I think she was very frightened."

"Thanks for rescuing her."

"When the fire started, she apparently got confused by the smoke. I heard her yelling."

"She's lucky you were around."

"Maybe." His sandy-blond eyebrows lowered into a straight line and his forehead pleated. "I think I need to invent a beeping system that's activated by smoke. Maybe something that's imbedded in the floor and leads a victim toward the exit."

Unable to resist the urge to touch him, to reassure herself that he was alive and well, Joanna palmed his cheek. "I think that would be a wonderful idea." If it worked and if the idea caught on, it might even earn him that million dollars he'd talked about.

"Sorry about your building," he said.

"Is the damage real bad?"

"Mostly the wall between Larry's and Percy's offices burned. The fire truck got here pretty fast."

"There's something about a hole in the roof, according to Bigelow."

"Yeah. How's your insurance?"

"Fine. Except that I have a huge deductible. It was all I could afford. Now this, plus the loan for the roof—"

"Look, I'm feeling a little guilty. I don't know if I'm the one who overloaded the circuits, but I do have some money. I'd like to—"

"I don't want your money, Kris. You need it to underwrite your next invention. Besides, I knew the wiring was old. The fire is my fault."

"No, really. I have more money than I could ever spend. I'd like you to—"

She hushed him by placing a finger on his lips. "You're sweet, Kris, and I truly appreciate your offer. But I've always been independent. I can't allow myself to be obligated to any man." Particularly one she loved. Her financial and family obligations were her own. She'd chosen to carry whatever burdens that entailed as a privilege, but she doubted a man would feel the same way. Tyler's father certainly hadn't, and his rejection still had the power to hurt. "I'll manage to get the repairs done." Though at the moment she wasn't quite sure how. Perhaps she could get a part-time job to make a little extra money. The supermarket was always looking for extra help and she knew the manager. She'd had his son in her class last year.

All the excitement had drawn a lot of onlookers. Cars had pulled off to the side of the road and kids on bikes milled around, gawking and jostling each other. Neighbors had appeared from their houses and were standing in clusters, visiting with one another.

Larry Smythe came marching through the crowd like a general bent on taking command.

"What the devil is going on here?" he asked.

"We had a small fire," Joanna said, pointing out the obvious. "The damage is minimal. Fortunately, Kris was here and called in the report. The fire truck responded very quickly."

Larry sniffed the air, looked appalled and covered his mouth and nose with a pristine white handkerchief. He stepped back a foot or two. "Toxic fumes," he muttered.

"I don't think so, Larry," Kris said. "You're smelling wood smoke and a little plastic insulation from the burned electrical wiring."

"Ah-ha. I knew those power surges meant trouble. You and your ridiculous inventions are responsible for this fire, Kris. And plastic fumes *are* toxic. I'm no fool. Everyone knows the dangers of plastics. There are wood finishes to be concerned about, too. And certain synthetics can be lethal. At the very least, a man could permanently damage his sinuses."

Kris said, "In an enclosed space, some plastics can be—"

"Don't worry, Larry," Joanna interjected. "I'll have the building aired out and the repairs made as quickly as possible. The disruption to your business will be very slight."

Eyes wide and fearful, he shook his head. "No, I couldn't possibly continue to work in that building. Toxins linger, you know. It might be months—or *years*—before it's safe to take a single breath in there. You never know about carcinogens. Or some residual poison that will attack your liver.'' His complexion turned slightly green at the prospect.

Mentally rolling her eyes, Joanna said, ''I understand your concerns, Larry, and if you feel you need to move out, naturally I'll refund your deposit.''

''Yes, yes, I'll appreciate that.'' His gaze darted from side to side, as if he expected some toxic dragon to dart out at him. ''I will need to remove my files. The furniture will be a total loss. Total. But perhaps I can find a way to sanitize my records.'' He hurried off, muttering something about sterilizing his files with ultraviolet light.

''You shouldn't give him back his money,'' Kris said. ''The guy's a nutcase. Once the building's been aired out, there won't be anything toxic left.''

''I know that, but the poor man would be miserable, assuming he stayed. Which I'm sure he wouldn't. Just talking about plastic fumes was making him green around the gills.''

''The fire could have as easily been his fault as mine. That darn air purifier of his required a lot of watts. You shouldn't have to give him back his money just because he's a hypochondriac. You need it more than he does.''

She rested her hand on his arm. ''Thanks for worrying about me. But I'll be all right.''

Kris wasn't quite as confident as Joanna was, at least when it came to her finances. A schoolteacher didn't earn much money, and she'd mentioned several times that she'd had problems getting a loan. If she wouldn't voluntarily accept his help, it appeared he'd have to take matters into his own hands.

He was at the bank when the doors opened the following morning.

Striding across the lobby, past old-fashioned teller windows and gleaming oak counters, he went directly to the bank president.

"Mr. Petersen, I'm Kris Slavik."

Smiling broadly, Wally Petersen stood and they shook hands. "Yes, sir, Mr. Slavik. Welcome to Sierra National Bank. My son indicated you'd be dropping by this morning."

"I should have transferred some of my funds here earlier, but I've been busy settling in." Kris took the chair the bank president offered. He knew his warm welcome was due in large measure to the clout that money confers on its owner. And Kris had lots and lots of clout when he chose to use it. "I assume you received the transfer of funds I ordered."

"Absolutely. First thing this morning. I must say, it is a more substantial sum than I had expected from what my son said about you. Nonetheless, your account is already open and now all we need is your signature on a few forms."

"Fine. There is something I will require in return for my deposit, however."

Wally Petersen raised eyebrows that were pencil thin. "Oh?"

"I believe Joanna Greer has applied here for a loan."

Petersen nodded cautiously.

"I would like Ms. Greer to receive her loan immediately, in whatever amount she requests."

The bank president propped his fingers together in front of his lips. "Ms. Greer is a charming woman, as you have no doubt noticed, but I do not consider the building she purchased to be a particularly good investment. Had the Forest Service continued its occupancy, my evaluation might have been different. And now, since there is also fire damage, I would not be a very good steward of my depositors' funds if I granted—"

"I don't believe I've made myself clear, Mr. Petersen. I am *guaranteeing* Ms. Greer's loan. If she defaults so much as a penny, you may deduct it from my account."

"I see."

"I also want Ms. Greer to believe the loan was made in the usual course of your business. She is not to know I am guaranteeing the funds."

"A most unusual arrangement."

"But terms you will agree to, Mr. Petersen, assuming you value me as a continuing customer of your bank."

"Oh, yes. Absolutely."

"Good." Kris smiled, leaned back and crossed one ankle over the other. He'd been in such a hurry to get to the bank that morning, he hadn't bothered to search through his things to find his socks, much less find a decent pair of jeans. Not that his appearance mattered. A seven-figure bank account spoke with great effect. Obviously, Mr. Petersen recognized that. "It would also be helpful if you could encourage whatever contractors she hires to hurry things along a bit. I'd hate for the rains to start before the repairs are completed.''

"Of course, Mr. Slavik. I'll see to matters myself.''

Kris thanked the bank president profusely for his assistance and returned to his car. His next stop would be the headquarters of Nanosoft Computerware Corporation.

Two hours later, he waved to the receptionist and, without signing in, rode the elevator up to the executive offices. Chad was on the phone, looking as dapper as ever in his silk suit and tie.

"I've got a little problem," Kris said when his former partner hung up.

"A technical problem?''

"Not exactly. There's a woman...''

"Ah. About time.'' A ridiculously self-satisfied smile stole across Chad's face. "You've come to the right man, ol' buddy. Sit down and tell me all about her.''

Joanna gazed in admiration at the new asphalt shingles that adorned her rental building. "It's amazing how fast Jason finished the job once he got started.'' It had only been a week since the fire, and even less time since she'd gotten the approval of her loan.

"You probably caught him at a good time, right between jobs,'' Kris told her.

She slid him an appreciative look. He was wearing

a blue-and-white polo shirt, new jeans and running shoes that looked as if they'd come right out of the box. He'd had a haircut, too. He cleaned up real good, as the saying went, but Joanna thought she might miss his long hair. Her fingers itched to test the new, shorter length. Mildly, she wondered why he'd taken such pains to spruce up a bit, then shrugged off the question. It was none of her business.

"I'm still trying to get over Wally Petersen actually calling me to say my loan had been approved. He said he'd heard about the fire and rushed the paperwork along."

"Maybe that's how the banking business works in a small town. He was probably being neighborly."

"I suppose. But it seems a little out of character for Mr. Petersen. More likely he knows about some large business that is planning to move into the area, which means my office building is suddenly worth more."

"Do I detect a note of cynicism in the lady's voice?" Kris teased.

Feeling more lighthearted than she had in a long time, she laughed. A new roof appeared to be an antidote to at least some of her malaise. The rest of her depression was obviously due to unrequited love, though she'd never dare admit that to anyone. Not even to herself, if she could help it. "I'm sorry. I should simply be happy that the loan finally came through. Now all I have to do is worry about paying it off. Which isn't going to be easy until I get Larry's office rented."

"You could jack up my rent. And Percy's. That would help."

Tucking her arm through his, she said, "That would be dishonest. You both have leases. I can't increase your rent for almost a whole year."

"And then you'll raise them?"

"Of course. I'm a greedy landlord who has her own bills to pay."

"Scrooge," he said in feigned accusation.

They walked from the front of the building to the rear, admiring the siding that Jason had replaced where the building was scorched. It had been cool all day and there was a hint of rain in the air. An old black oak behind the building had finally begun to change color, the leaves turning a bright yellow that the late afternoon sun caught in its waning glow. The loan had arrived just in time, Joanna mused. Maybe she owed a debt of thanks to whatever had overloaded the circuits and caused the fire.

When they returned to the parking lot, she saw her mother crossing the street toward them with a white-haired gentleman in a business suit at her side.

"Yoo-hoo, dear," Agnes called, waving. "There you are." She seemed particularly spry, stepping lightly over a shallow drainage ditch that carried rain runoff from the roadway. The gentleman caught her elbow to steady her, and Agnes used her free hand to hike up her flowing skirt.

"Hello, Mother. I was on my way home—"

"You remember Herbert Parkin, don't you, dear?"

Studying the gentleman, Joanna got the impression

of clear-eyed intelligence and wonderful good health. "I'm sorry, I don't recall—"

"You were about ten the last time I saw you, my dear. With pigtails and skinned knees. I must say, you've grown into a lovely young woman. Much like your mother was at your age."

Joanna flushed.

"He was a friend of your father's, dear. They went to school together."

"I was your friend, too, Agnes."

Her mother's cheeks pinked as thoroughly as Joanna's had. "Yes, I know that, Herbert. But I did date Alexander all through high school."

"To my great regret. You never gave me a second look."

Agnes tittered. "Oh, go on with you. You had more girls than you could manage as it was. You weren't interested in me."

Wondering just exactly what was going on, Joanna introduced Kris. "He rents the end office and the garage. He's an inventor," she explained.

The two men shook hands and in the process took each other's measure.

"Nice to meet you," Kris said. "Mrs. Greer is one of my favorite people. She's also a hell of a good cook who is kind enough to invite me to dinner from time to time."

"I haven't been so favored in a long while." Herbert glanced at Agnes. "Perhaps if I hint broadly enough, she'll invite me as well."

"Pshaw, Herbert. You know you're welcome. You always have been." Agnes patted his arm. "Dear

Herbert lost his wife only a year ago. They lived in San Francisco. Now he's thinking about moving back to the mountains.''

"I'm thinking of retiring here, as a matter of fact."

"What business are you in?'' Kris asked.

"Stocks. Turner, Parkin and Joiner. Maybe you know the firm?"

"As it happens, I do. Specialists in venture capital. A very successful record, as I recall. It seems to me your company handled the first sale of Nanosoft stock when the company went public."

Herbert tilted his head to the side and studied Kris a moment. "We did indeed. I wrote the prospectus myself, in cooperation with the company's president for business affairs—Chad Harris. Our efforts were very successful, and the return for those who purchased the initial offering was excellent."

"Yes, I know."

"In my opinion, NCC's technical expertise was unparalleled."

Kris's smile was extremely wide and matched by that of Mr. Parkin. Joanna wondered at the sudden warmth between the two men.

"Herbert wanted to see our vacant office," her mother said.

That surprised Joanna, since he'd just indicated he was planning to retire.

In response to her unspoken question, Herbert said, "Several of my clients want me to continue to advise them regarding their portfolios even after I officially retire. Given faxes and E-mail, it matters little if my office is in San Francisco or here." Patrician and dignified, he glanced again at Agnes. The corners of his eyes crinkled as he smiled. "Though I can see a great many benefits to living in the Twain Harte area."

"I've found my retirement here to be very pleasant," Kris said. "I could add that the Greer ladies are fine landlords."

Sensing messages being sent and received that she couldn't quite translate, Joanna invited Herbert to take a look at Larry's recently vacated office. She hoped Mr. Parkin wasn't getting any romantic notions about her mother, not at their age. Though it appeared her mother was particularly lucid this afternoon, almost effervescent, it was another of her purple days, and she'd recently colored her hair. The shade was closer to a shocking violet than to a subdued blue-gray that a hair stylist would have chosen. Neither Kris nor Herbert seemed to notice or care.

"This will do very nicely," Herbert announced after only a cursory examination of the office.

"Lovely!" Agnes hooked her arm through his. "You can come back home with me, and I'll find the lease forms for you to sign."

"I trust you'll give me a discounted rate, for old time's sake."

"Nonsense, dear boy. I plan to double the rent and fully expect you to eat up my outlandish profits by dining with us at every opportunity."

"It will be my pleasure."

Nonplussed, Joanna watched the two of them go out the door arm in arm, as if they were a couple of adolescents embarking on their first date.

"Like mother, like daughter," Kris said with a laugh. "Trying to take advantage of their tenants."

"I'm more worried that Mr. Parkin might be... well, there are men who take advantage of older women who they think have a little money." Joanna had once thought Kris might be that kind of a Lothario, though she'd since had a change of heart.

He slid his arm around her shoulders. "I don't think you have to worry about that when it comes to Herbert. He could probably buy up half of San Francisco and it wouldn't even put a dent in his pocketbook."

"Really? You really know him?"

"I certainly know *of* him. He's among the best at what he does."

In that case, Joanna ought to be worrying about her mother for another reason. When Mr. Parkin realized just how eccentric Agnes had become, he might well break her heart.

Sliding a glance toward Kris, Joanna decided she wouldn't be able to handle that sort of rejection of her family a second time.

By the end of the week, however, she was wishing all kinds of dire consequences on Isabel and Paul Currant, not Herbert Parkin. The coaches had ducked out on the football team again. This time they were enjoying a second honeymoon in some secluded locale while the team played its final game of the season. An *important* game.

"Don't they know children need a sense of stability?" Joanna muttered under her breath as she arrived at the field shortly before game time. "Adults ought to *care* what happens to their kids."

Kris appeared with his usual armload of books and dropped them to the ground. "I've been talking with the other coaches. I think we can beat this team with a couple of trick plays I have up my sleeve."

Curious about the source of his newfound football wisdom, she glanced down at the books. The first two titles leaped up at her—*The Language of Romance* and *Courtship in the Nineties.* The breath was driven from her lungs and her head snapped up again. What kind of football strategy was that?

"See, I'm thinking about a double reverse," he continued, unaware of her reaction. "Assuming we're somewhere near their thirty or so, I think it may work. They're a swarming team and they'll overrun the play to the wrong side. What do you think?"

Think? She couldn't possibly think. Not about football. She wanted to know who he was courting. Was she the one? Or had he met someone else? That possibility terrified her. Which wasn't fair. He had a right—

Struggling against a wretched need to burst into tears, she swallowed hard. "I think it's better if we keep it simple and just encourage the boys to play the very best they can," she said.

His expression clouded with disappointment that his grand plan hadn't met with her approval. "Really? There's also a fake handoff and a fullback pass that looked like they might have possibilities."

"Unless the team has practiced the plays, simple is better."

He shrugged. "Okay. You know more about football than I do."

She didn't. Not really, given the fact he'd been reading up on the subject. Nor did she know all that much about courtship. Certainly not in the nineties. The last time she'd been out on a date had been years ago, and that had been a fiasco.

Courtship in the nineties was as much a mystery to her as smart-bomb technology. And just as dangerous.

The game commenced and progressed without much help from Joanna. She cheered or groaned at appropriate moments, offered cold drinks to the boys along with encouragement. She even sent in a quarterback draw play at one point. But her thoughts were mostly on the reference books Kris had brought to the game. They lay there on the ground near the bench, mocking her. Tempting her. Making her crazy.

What was he up to? And why? Not that she hadn't been aware he was attracted to her, but now he seemed to have turned up the heat. She certainly felt a flush that couldn't be accounted for by the cool autumn air. She desperately wanted his attention to be directed at her, feared there might be another woman and knew—in either case—she wasn't being fair.

One thing she knew for sure, Kris Slavik had tunnel vision when he was working on a project. If he'd decided to go courting, that was what he'd do. With a vengeance. If she was the object of his interest, and he decided to bring to bear the full weight of his intellect and sexy charm, she would be hard-pressed to resist his efforts.

She needed to. The past had taught her a heart was a fragile thing, easily damaged.

With less than a minute to go in the game and their team down by four points, Kris called a time-out. He signaled the offensive players to come to the sidelines.

"What are you up to?" Joanna asked.

"If we're going to win this game, it's now or never. I'm going to send in the halfback pass."

"You think Cody is up to it?"

"I'm going to give him a chance."

He gathered the boys around him, and together they studied the diagram in the coaching book. Breaking the huddle, he said, "Okay, guys, make it look like a run and make it good."

Joanna held her breath as the team lined up on the thirty-yard line. Tyler took his place behind the center. He gave it a long count, but nobody jumped off-side. The play started in slow motion, with Tyler handing off the ball off to Cody, who ran to the right, two defensive players in hot pursuit.

The pass Cody hefted toward the end zone was a perfect spiral.

"Man, I wish I could pass like that," Kris said as the ball arched overhead. "He's a real pro."

"I hope that Dunlap boy can catch like a pro."

The action speeded up as the receiver jumped for the ball at the same time a defender arrived. They went into the air together. The ball bounced back up like a volleyball. Another defender dove for the falling projectile. He juggled it, then pulled it into his midsection as he tumbled to the ground.

Interception.

A chorus of groans rose from their side of the field and victory cheers came from across the way.

Dejected, Tyler, Cody and the rest of the offense came off the field.

"Great play, guys," Kris said. He slapped backs and patted helmets. "Perfect throw, Cody."

"Yeah, but we lost, Coach. All they have to do is kneel down and the game's over."

"Hey, you gave it a shot and played hard. You're winners. Every one of you."

Tyler looked up at Kris. "Does that mean we get pizza even if we didn't win the league?"

"You bet, son. All the pizza you want, and it's on me."

Emotion crowding in her chest, Joanna closed her eyes tight as the final gun sounded. She wanted to hug Tyler and Cody and Kris but didn't think any of them would appreciate a public display of affection. And the fact was, she wanted to do far more than hug Kris.

Offering a lame excuse about being too tired, she made her escape and headed for home while the rest of the team went for pizza.

She walked into her living room and was struck by an incredible floral scent. Curious, she looked around.

"Aren't they wonderful?" Her mother appeared

with an armload of red roses. "Herbert sent them. Isn't he sweet?"

"Yes, he's..." Joanna's heart plummeted. She'd had no right to expect—

"There's another bouquet for you, dear."

"From Herbert?"

Fussing with her flowers, Agnes arranged them in a crystal vase, then stood back to admire her work. "I sneaked a peek at the card, dear. I hope you don't mind."

"No, of course not." Joanna clenched her teeth. Any minute now she was going to start screaming. Where were the flowers? Who were they from? Naturally, she didn't want to upset her mother, but there were limits...

"There's a gift with your flowers, wrapped up nice with a bow 'n' all. I didn't look at that. I didn't think it was my place."

"Mother! What flowers? Where?"

Her eyelids fluttered. "In your room, of course. Where else would I put them?"

Joanna lost all sense of composure. She raced to her room and burst inside.

The bouquet wasn't roses but a natural array of autumn leaves interspersed with branches heavy with ripe blackberries. The composition had been arranged with exquisite care in a hand-thrown vase.

Herbert hadn't sent this bouquet. No one but Kris would have known about her love of blackberries. Nor would they have been meaningful to anyone else.

With a scrawled signature, the card confirmed she was right.

Kris.

She sank to the edge of her bed. He shouldn't have done this. He shouldn't have been so thoughtful. A man shouldn't have the power to touch her so deeply.

With shaking fingers she retrieved the small package that nestled among the leaves. A book, she realized as she stripped the wrapping away.

Shakespearean sonnets.

Kris knew about electronics and computers, odd bits of trivia and high-tech stuff that Joanna could barely comprehend. What he had chosen as a gift meant he'd been listening to her with his heart, not only with his brilliant mind.

No present could have meant more.

And no gift could have made her ache so to reach for dreams she had once set aside.

She sat in her room for a long time. Tyler came home, shouted something and banged out the door again. Inside, the house it was silent; outside, cars hummed by on the highway that fronted her rental property—Kris's office and workshop included.

Joanna's heart warred with her head. Every time her emotions managed to gain the winning edge, her mind countered with myriad insurmountable problems that arose like ghosts from a graveyard.

She shook off her mental paralysis.

She had to thank Kris for his thoughtful gift. Whatever her emotional dilemma, he deserved that common courtesy.

Chapter Nine

The cool evening air sent gooseflesh down her arms as she crossed the street, or maybe her sudden chill was a result of anxiety and indecision.

The light was on in his office, his workshop dark. How did he live? she wondered.

Never once had she been in the office since he had rented the property, yet she knew that was where he slept and ate at least some of his meals. Camping out, as he'd told her mother. A strange curiosity nudged at her awareness. She wanted to know the intimate details of his life. Was he messy or neat? Did he make his bed in the mornings? Was the bed large enough for two?

Closing her eyes, she drew a deep breath. That was *not* a question she should be asking.

She walked up the steps onto the porch and knocked. A moment later he opened the door. Without conscious thought, her gaze slid past him.

Unmade and plenty big enough for two.

She swallowed thickly. "I wanted to thank you for the...floral arrangement."

"The florist thought I should have sent roses."

"No. It was perfect. Unique." Like the man. "Thank you. For the sonnets, too. They're lovely."

"You're welcome." He shifted his feet uneasily and lifted his shoulders in an awkward shrug. "You want to come in?"

"Maybe. For just a minute." *Fool, fool,* she told herself. She'd thanked him. Now she should leave. But like a powerful magnet, the interior of the room drew her. Her pulse stuttered. "If you aren't busy."

"No. Not at all. I was just reading some technical journals. Boring stuff." He opened the door wider and she stepped across the threshold.

Kris caught the subtle fragrance of her perfume and he wondered at its power to arouse. Biological response to various aromas was beyond his area of expertise, but in Joanna's case he didn't need specific information. His body simply reacted. Forcefully.

"Interesting decor," she commented dryly.

His gaze circled the room, seeing the clutter for the first time through the eyes of a stranger. What little furniture he had was totally mismatched, and most of it was covered with discarded clothing or books and magazines he'd set aside. Not an impressive sight, he realized, and he did want to impress Joanna. "I got the bed at the consignment store in town."

In a tentative caress, her fingertips traced the curving shape of the post at the foot of the bed. "Yes, I remember seeing it in the window. Brass is nice."

"The mattress and springs are new. I like a firm mattress."

A smile teased at the corners of her lips. "So do I."

Kris began to sweat. "Here, let me clear off a place for you to sit." He hauled the only chair in the room away from the desk, dumped the stack of books it held onto the floor, turned it around and brushed the dust from the seat with his hand. "Neat's never been my long suit."

"I can see that."

"Joanna..." He cleared his throat and his gaze hurtled toward the unmade bed.

Her eyes widened and she followed the direction of his glance. "I really can't stay. I just wanted to thank you."

Damn, he was doing this all wrong. Chad had told him to change his image if he wanted to attract a woman. New jeans and a designer polo shirt weren't enough. Kris should have had a palace for Joanna to visit, not a made-over office that looked as if a family of pack rats had taken up residence.

He tried to think what Chad would do in his place. Hooking his thumbs in his jean pockets, Kris took a couple of sauntering steps toward Joanna. Think macho, he told himself.

Frowning, she cocked her head. "Is there something wrong?"

"Yeah." *Him.* He was thinking too much when all he wanted was to act on his instincts.

In one more long stride, he closed the distance between them and pulled her into his arms. She groaned softly as he covered her lips with his. She tasted both sweet and seductive, a dizzying combination that set his body on fire. He wanted this woman as he had never wanted any other woman before. Holding her close, his palm pressing against the swell of her hips, he let her feel how much he wanted her.

She nestled against him as if they were two halves designed to fit together, hard against soft, curves and angles matching perfectly. Yep, superior engineering, he thought in admiration as he deepened the kiss.

As Joanna's hands crept up Kris's chest and linked behind his neck, she felt herself losing the battle with her good sense. One by one, concerns she'd clung to for years were replaced with issues of far more urgency—the warmth of his palm sliding up her back beneath her sweater. The insistent press of his arousal. A determined need that thrummed through her, seeking release.

She shouldn't be doing this, she shouldn't be wanting this and yet she was helpless to stop. In some corner of her heart, she desperately wanted to believe all of this could be real—that happy endings could happen.

In an agony of self-doubt and indecision, she broke the kiss.

His eyes had turned to a deep pewter, like tarnished silver. "It would be good between us."

"I know." The knowledge filled her awareness, making her voice husky. He had the power to excite her and make her forget like no other man she had ever met. As a lover, he would be exquisite.

"I didn't mean to rush you."

"You didn't." She was ready, perhaps foolishly so. Her knees were rubbery with wanting.

A sharp knock sounded on the door.

Joanna jumped. A reprieve, she thought. Almost too late. Or hours too soon. "I forgot to tell Mother where I was going."

Kris swore softly under his breath. "You open it." Turning his back, he added, "At the moment, I'm not exactly in good shape to make small talk with your mother."

Neither was Joanna. Her face was flushed and her heart pulsed heavily. She suspected her lips might well reveal they'd been recently and soundly kissed.

Taking a deep breath, she responded to a second knock.

It wasn't her mother. It was Percy with a friend.

"I saw your light on—oh, you're here, too, Joanna." Percy smiled delightedly. "That's perfect. I wanted you both to meet Imogene. We're..." A flush crept up his cheeks. "She and I...we're going steady. We haven't actually known each other long enough yet to become engaged."

"Th-that's wonderful," Joanna stammered, taken aback by the stab of envy that sliced through her. Why was she the only one asked to step into the ark without a partner?

The woman with Percy was about his height and had the same narrow-faced look. What she lacked in a perfect figure, she easily made up for with a radiant smile and glorious red hair.

"My mother's very pleased." Obviously, so was Percy. The buttons on his suit jacket were practically popping as his chest swelled with pride.

"I'm sure she is."

"I took a page from your book, Joanna. I advertised!"

"Really? How clever of you." Joanna glanced over her shoulder at Kris. Based on the possessive look in his eyes, she could tell their relationship had subtly shifted. He knew she had come very close to going to bed with him. From now on, it would only be a question of time. No doubt he would develop a new strategy based on extensive research, one she couldn't resist. On the other hand, it wouldn't take a rocket scientist or a genius to realize she had already tumbled into love.

Kris joined her at the door, trying to make the best of an awkward situation. "Why don't you two come on in? I've probably got a beer or two. We can celebrate." The mood had been broken, he realized. Besides, he figured he'd already lost his chance to coax Joanna into his bed. This time.

Imogene smiled shyly. "We really can't. Percival's mother is expecting us. She's such a dear lady. I lost my mother when I was only nine and it's almost like finding her again." She tucked her arm through Percy's. "Should we go now, poopsie?"

"Whatever you'd like, sweetums."

"I was just on my way home, too," Joanna said

with a little too much haste. "I'll walk with you to your car."

Kris caught her hand. "You don't have to go. It's early."

Her fleeting moment of indecision gave him hope, even when she murmured, "I think it's better if we both take a little time to think."

Without breaking eye contact, she pulled her fingers from his grasp. And then she was out the door.

Watching Joanna escape in the company of the two lovebirds, he conceded Chad was right. Kris had to totally change his image and bring a whole lot of clout to bear on the problem. He needed to project himself as the best damn catch this side of the Mississippi, possibly in the entire universe.

Fortunately, he enjoyed a challenge.

He frowned and stuffed his hands in his pockets. In frustration, he ground his teeth together. Maybe roses would have been better.

Damn! Computing advanced quantum theories was simple compared to courting a woman. Or maybe, he thought with an uncharacteristic lack of self-confidence, he didn't have the right stuff as far as Joanna was concerned.

Joanna didn't have a jealous bone in her body.

The sight of two unfamiliar cars and one gorgeous blonde talking to Kris in the parking lot of the rental property was not why she wheeled her vehicle into a right turn instead of going on home after school. She simply hadn't seen Kris in a couple of days and thought she'd say hello.

Yeah, sure. And jack-o'-lanterns grow on trees.

Trying to appear casual, she parked and took her time getting out of the car.

"Come on over," Kris called. "There's someone I want you to meet."

That was encouraging. If it was "the other woman," he wouldn't be so eager to introduce her. Joanna still wasn't too thrilled with him talking to an attractive female with long legs and perfectly styled hair, who looked as if she'd just come from her modeling job in San Francisco.

His cheek creased with a smile as Joanna approached and he held out his hand. She took it. Whoever this woman was, Joanna was going to make sure her claim was well staked out.

"Joanna, this is my sister, Rochelle. Sis, meet my landlady, Joanna Greer."

Relief swept over Joanna and she chided herself for indulging in a childish emotion like jealousy. Kris was a free man. If he wanted to see other women, he was perfectly within his rights to do so. She was, however, inordinately pleased to discover this stunning woman was his sibling.

"Nice to meet you," Joanna said, meaning it.

"My pleasure." Shaking hands, Rochelle met her gaze with the same gray-eyed intelligence as her brother. But at the moment she lacked his dazzling smile.

"Joanna lives across the street."

His sister's gaze followed the direction Kris indicated. Rochelle raised disapproving eyebrows. "Not

the house with all those ridiculous whirligigs on top,
I hope.''

Joanna tensed. "My father made them.''

"Yeah, aren't they great?'' Kris said. "I've been
trying to figure out how to harness all that wind
power.''

"You're certainly determined to waste your talents, big brother.''

With an unconcerned shrug, Kris said, "Rochelle's come to bawl me out.''

It was Joanna's turn to raise her eyebrows. "All
the way from MIT?''

"Our parents have been concerned about Kristopher. I had a little free time, so they asked me to
drop by.''

Odd, Joanna thought, that his parents wouldn't
check up on him themselves, but she'd already realized he hadn't been raised in a particularly affectionate family. His sister had apparently inherited the
same trait.

Kris looped his arm across Joanna's shoulder. "It
seems our parents believe I have gone to wrack and
ruin by moving up here to the mountains.''

"It was bad enough when you gave up your brilliant research career to start your own company.
Now...'' Rochelle glanced around at the rustic setting with obvious disdain. "You've buried yourself
so far back in the woods that you might as well be
living in the Ukraine. How can you expect to live up
to your potential, to make any sort of contribution to
society if you waste your talents in some place so
totally lacking in academic stimulation?''

"That sounds like a direct quote from Mother," Kris said.

"Excuse me?" Joanna bristled. She'd had about enough of Rochelle's condescending attitude. "Kris's brilliant mind made it possible for a blind boy to ride in a mountain-bike race that he'd dreamed about but never thought he'd have a chance to even participate in. I think that's quite a contribution to our little backwoods community."

Rochelle arched perfectly shaped eyebrows. "One boy? With Kris's talents, he should be tackling problems of worldwide importance."

"You should have seen that youngster's smile when he crossed the finish line." Joanna's dander was really up now. Imagine anyone criticizing Kris after what he had done for Peter. "I bet none of your robots ever made so much difference in one child's life."

"The robotics I'm working on will revolutionize industrial technology for years to come."

"Rochelle's even smarter than I am," Kris conceded easily.

"That's wonderful," Joanna stated. "I'm impressed, and I'm sure her work is very important. But we also need people like you who will go out of your way to change the world for one child at a time."

"Yes, of course." Rochelle didn't look convinced. "Well, Kris, dear, I suppose you'll do what you want, in any event. You always have." With a shake of her head, she shot another disapproving glance toward the rooftop of whirligigs. To Joanna she said, "Perhaps we'll meet again."

"I don't get to Boston often."

"No, I don't suppose you do." She brushed Kris's cheek with a kiss that was more air than substance. "Behave yourself, Kristopher. You'll be welcome back in the fold whenever you're ready."

He grinned as his sister got into the car. "Tell Mother and Dad you did your best."

Still upset by Rochelle's attitude, Joanna was not sorry to see the young woman leave. But Joanna had learned something important. If she weakened and let her heart rule her head, she'd be setting herself up for a fall, and Kris, too. His parents would never approve of her and the sometimes peculiar antics of Agnes. Rochelle had made that abundantly clear.

"Thanks," Kris said.

Joanna drew her gaze away from the departing car and looked up into Kris's eyes. "For what?"

"For defending me. Not many people are courageous enough to challenge my sister on anything."

"Well, she's wrong, that's all, and she really made me mad. I couldn't stand idly by while she badgered you about having started a company that failed. At least you tried."

"You really don't care what I do for a living, do you?"

"Of course not. As long as you don't rob banks." Which was a possibility Joanna had considered that first day they'd met, when he'd peeled off all those hundred-dollar bills.

"Joanna, my company didn't fail."

"It didn't? But you're not working—"

"I retired from Nanosoft Computerware, the fastest-growing software company in the world. That's the firm I founded.''

"Nanosoft," she echoed. "That's how you got those computers donated to the school."

"Yep. Founders still have a certain amount of pull even after they retire."

Confused, Joanna found her mental gears moving slowly and with little precision. If he was founder of Nanosoft, he ought to be worth megabucks, but he lived as if he had to manage every dime frugally. After all, he had a consignment-store bed, an entire wardrobe that until recently consisted of tattered jeans, and an equally dilapidated car.

She frowned. Where was his car? The only one left in the lot beside hers was a new utility sport vehicle with the dealer's sticker still in the window.

As if he'd read her mind, Kris ushered her toward the forest green Blazer. "Come on. I'll take you for a ride."

"This is yours?"

"Yep. I'm in the process of changing my image. It was time I gave the Oldsmobile a decent burial. It's been terminal for a long time."

The new vehicle looked more than ready to make up for whatever the old junker had lacked.

Joanna settled into the seat, inhaling the tantalizing scent of newness and luxury as soft leather embraced her. She fastened the seat belt.

"You don't believe in half measures, do you?" she commented. From the looks of it, he hadn't skipped a single option, including air-conditioning and four-wheel drive.

"I did a little research." He turned the key in the ignition. "All things considered, this car seemed to fit my needs best."

"And you could afford it?"

He slanted her a glance, amusement crinkling the corners of his eyes. "Easily."

"I see." Actually, she didn't see at all. Had he been intentionally hiding the fact that he had money? Lots of it? "Did you make up that story about being an inventor?"

"Not exactly. I personally hold the copyrights on a bunch of software programs. When I told you I was an inventor, I figured you'd be more impressed with that than if I said I was a computer hacker. Besides, I did think it'd be worth it if I could get you on a dual bike with me."

"That didn't work out quite as you had in mind."

"Maybe I'll try again sometime."

As he drove, she studied him with increasing curiosity. One part of her mind acknowledged she knew very little of his past; the other part simply admired the man he had become. She'd never considered money an issue one way or the other when it came to her romantic relationship with a man. It was the emotional burden of an aging and eccentric relative that was difficult to accept, although the road to bankruptcy was no doubt daunting to most travelers charged with the care of another. She had that problem to look forward to with her mother.

Though recently, Joanna mused—since Herbert Parkin had arrived in town—Agnes's mind had seemed particularly keen. She and her new beau had been out almost every night, and when they weren't together they talked on the phone for hours. It was driving Tyler crazy that he couldn't call his friends unless Grandma was out of the house.

Maybe Joanna's fears were unfounded.

Kris had followed a series of winding roads through the forest. They led, she discovered, to an upscale development of newer homes, each one boasting a five-acre-minimum lot and three-thousand square feet of living space, not to mention oversize garages and an occasional outbuilding. He pulled into a circular driveway.

"Why are we stopping here?" she asked.

"I spent some time the last few days with a realtor. I spotted a couple of houses I kind of like and I wanted your opinion."

Her eyes widened. "You're thinking about buying this?" The house was a sprawling two-story ranch style with brick accents and neatly trimmed lawns and flower beds. Beyond the split-rail fence of the formal yard the surrounding landscape was as nature intended, with pines, cedars and oaks, plus the autumn-dried remains of wildflowers. From the back of the house there would be a view of the mountains to the south and the valley to the west. She'd guess the value of the property exceeded a million dollars. The thought stunned her.

"Percy said I shouldn't pay cash. It'd be better to borrow the money so I can get a write-off on my taxes. He thinks I ought to talk to Herbert Parkin, too, about sheltering some of my money."

"I've never had that problem." Her money drained away before she had a chance to shelter it.

"The house is vacant. I don't have a key, but we can walk around to take a closer look."

He helped her out of the truck, then slid his arm possessively around her waist, setting up a warm and needy response low in her body. She had the oddest feeling, as if they were a couple checking out a honeymoon cottage. Except this was more nearly a mansion, far larger than any home she had ever dreamed of owning.

"I know it's none of my business—and you can certainly tell me so—but just how wealthy are you? In round figures."

They arrived at an expansive redwood deck that provided a view of the Sierra foothills. The afternoon sun was low, shadowing the valleys between ridges in a soft purple haze. On a clear morning she'd be able to see almost as far as Yosemite, and every evening this deck would be the last place the sun would abandon. It simply took her breath away.

"Depending on market prices and rounding off, I'd say I'm worth something over twenty million."

"Twenty—" She choked. Her gaze whipped back to Kris. "You're kidding."

"That's why I retired. I couldn't imagine ever needing more money than that."

Neither could Joanna. Not in her wildest dreams.

"Why didn't you tell me you were incredibly rich?"

"Would it have made a difference how you felt about me?"

"No." She'd fallen in love with the man, not his money. "I promise I wouldn't have held your money against you."

His intimate chuckle was low and throaty, inviting company.

One of those dreams that Joanna had suppressed long ago nudged its way to the surface again—a husband for her, a father for Tyler, a way to care for her mother. But more importantly, the freedom to love one special man.

This was a house where a family could grow and thrive—young children tumbling on the grass out front or playing hide-and-seek among the trees; adolescent friends of Tyler sharing the pain of becoming adults here on the deck as they barbecued hamburgers and watched a setting sun. And all the while the house would be filled with laughter and love, filled with Kris's bright, inquisitive sons and daughters.

He brushed a kiss to her forehead. "So what do you think?"

Sudden tears of happiness pressed at the back of her eyes. "I think it's perfect."

"The other house I liked doesn't have a view, but it's bigger and closer to town."

"Big isn't necessarily better, except when it comes to views. This is truly extraordinary. You'd never tire of looking at it."

"That's kind of what I thought."

They stood in silence, simply absorbing the grandeur together until the sun dipped behind a bank of dark clouds to the west. Almost immediately the temperature dropped by several degrees and there was the scent of rain in the air. Joanna shivered.

"I'd better get home and check on Tyler. Since the football season ended he's been at loose ends."

Still feeling the glow of warmth that came from love and didn't require the sun, Joanna watched the shadows deepen beneath the pines as they drove down the hill to Twain Harte. Within fifteen minutes, Kris pulled the Blazer into the parking lot next to her car.

She was just getting out when she heard, "Mom! Mom! Where have you been? I've been waiting forever!"

Fear sliced through her. "What is it, Tyler?"

"It's Grandma! She was trying out my snowboard on the back hill. On the dry pine needles. It was crazy." He looked wild-eyed. "She fell, Mom. Real hard."

"Where is she?"

"I called 9-1-1. I didn't know what else to do."

"You did fine, son. Calm down and tell me what happened."

"They came and got her, Mom. In an ambulance. They said I should wait for you. She was..." His chin trembled. "They couldn't wake her up."

Chapter Ten

She hated hospitals.

Even the lobby smelled medicinal. As she rode up in the elevator, the intensity of her fears grew in direct proportion to the number of floors.

Too many times in Joanna's life she'd come to this hospital to receive the news that someone she loved had died—first her grandmother and then, only a few years later, her father. The weight of those memories pressed down on her along with all the accompanying grief as she stepped out onto the third floor. Kris and her son were right beside her.

"Easy, Joanna." Kris placed a reassuring hand at her waist. "You look like you're going to pass out."

Tension twisted knots in her stomach. "I'm fine."

"Is Grandma going to be all right, Mom?" Tyler asked.

"We'll see, honey. I hope so."

They were hurrying down the corridor when

Royce Morgan, the Greers' longtime family physician, appeared.

"Ah, Joanna, my dear. And young Tyler." The balding man clasped her hands. "I'm glad you're here. Both of you."

"How is she, Doctor?"

"Holding her own, I'd say." He glanced briefly at Kris and nodded a greeting. "She's twisted her knee rather badly, but there's no break. And she does have a nasty bruise on her head to go along with her concussion."

"Is it serious?"

"I suppose at her age any concussion could be considered serious. And she was just plain lucky she didn't break her hip." He shook his head in dismay. "Why would she pull a stunt like that—snowboarding?"

"But she's going to be all right?" Joanna persisted.

"I expect she'll need some physical therapy for that knee. And a shrink for her head years ago might have been helpful." He smiled, his regard for his patient's quirks both kindly and affectionate. "But yes, she'll be fine."

Joanna's shoulders sagged in relief and the tension drained from her. "Thank you, Doctor."

"I am somewhat more troubled by her confused state of mind at the moment," he continued. "The last few times she's been to my office, she seemed…well, at her age early signs of senility are possible. And given her family history… This concussion may have exacerbated an existing problem."

Dr. Morgan's gentle, caring words pierced Joanna's heart like double-edged swords. *Senility?* Her mother was too young, too vital, for that, however eccentric she might seem to others.

"May I see her?" Joanna asked, her throat closing tight from her fears.

"Yes, of course, my dear. One at a time, if you will. And don't stay long. Most of all, she needs her rest."

Joanna hesitated a moment, until Tyler said, "You go ahead, Mom. I'll wait with Kris."

"Thanks, honey." Though she felt anything but confident, she gave Tyler a reassuring hug. "I'll tell her you send your love."

Kris brushed his fingertips to her cheek. "We'll be here when you're through. Give Agnes a kiss from me, too."

She tried to thank him, but the words simply wouldn't slide past the lump in her throat, so she nodded instead. Her eyes blurred with tears. Such a good man, a kind man, and he deserved more than the burden she had to carry. For a few brief minutes she had let love blind her to that truth.

Joanna stepped into her mother's room. The IV dangling from a pole sent a ripple of fear through her. Agnes's gray pallor was in shocking contrast to her tinted hair. In that instant, Joanna was swept with love and the knowledge that life was a very precarious and precious commodity.

"Mother?" Whispering, she clasped her mother's hand and brought it to her lips.

Agnes's eyes fluttered open. Her weak, lopsided smile nearly broke Joanna's heart.

"Is your father coming, dear?" Her speech was slurred.

"Father?"

"Alexander. He said he might be late for supper."

The band around Joanna's chest pulled taut and constricted her breathing. "You mustn't worry about Dad." Bending down, she kissed her mother's forehead. "Dr. Morgan says you'll be fine in no time, but that now you need to rest."

"Tired. Very tired. I have such a terrible headache. I wish your father..."

"I know, Mama. I know." Stroking her mother's hand, Joanna waited and watched until Agnes drifted back to sleep, her breathing settling into an even rhythm. The tears that had clogged Joanna's throat leaked out to dampen her cheeks. She knew what had to be done. Once again, her dreams had to be set aside. This time forever.

It was nearly midnight when the nurses convinced Joanna that her mother would be fine for the rest of the night, and that she needed to get her son to bed.

Kris drove them home over roads slick with the rain that had begun to fall while they were at the hospital. The dark, dismal night suited Joanna's mood. Even the scattered streetlights gave little illumination through the heavy sheets of rain.

Staggering with fatigue, Tyler stumbled as he entered the house. "Mom, can I stay home tomorrow and go see Grandma again?" he asked, bleary-eyed.

"We'll see, son. Right now what you need to do is go to bed."

Feet shuffling, he went off down the hallway to his room.

"You look like you could use about twelve hours straight of sleep yourself," Kris said.

He pulled her into his arms. She resisted briefly, then realized she desperately needed to feel his strength one last time. He was such a solid man, both physically and intellectually, that she wanted to lean on him. But that wasn't fair. She remembered so clearly the last conversation she'd had with Tyler's father.

"Your whole family is screwy," Nate said, his dark eyebrows lowered into a sneer. "You know what the other kids call you? The 'Whirligig Kid,' that's what. My folks would have a fit if I married you."

"If I'm such a terrible person, why did you bother to date me?" Much less go to so much trouble that she'd fall in love, Joanna thought frantically.

"You're sexy, babe. I wanted to get into your pants."

Appalled, she stepped back. "That's all you wanted? But you told me—"

"Look, babe, why would any guy want to saddle himself with your family? Your grandma's totally weird, and your folks aren't much better. I'd guess the older you get the more like that old biddy you'll become. I don't want any part of it."

"But the baby?" The question rasped like razor blades in her throat.

"Do whatever you want with the kid. I'm outta here."

Now, Joanna's mother, who might well be sliding into senility, would need more care than ever. And her slipping around on a snowboard was sure and certain confirmation of Nate's accusations. The Greer family was terribly eccentric.

Kris brushed a sweet and gentle kiss on her forehead. "I know my timing is off and I know you're worried about your mother, but if you really like that house with a view, I think I ought to make an offer. I wouldn't want anyone to beat me to it."

A terrible paralysis gripped Joanna, a pain far more severe than anything she'd previously experienced. How could she let this man go?

How could she not?

Reaching past fatigue and heartbreak, she plumbed her very depths for the courage to do what was right. Palming his chest, she took a step back.

"The choice is yours, Kris. You'll be the one living there, not me."

"But I thought—"

"With Mother so ill, that's all I can think about now. Assuming all goes well, she'll be coming home in the next few days and will need a great deal of care. On top of my teaching, I won't have the time or energy for anything else."

His brows lowered. "What are you saying?"

She raised her gaze to meet his straight on. The look of hurt she saw was worse than she could have possibly imagined, and it tore at her. But she was doing this for him, not for herself. "I'm saying..." In spite of everything, the lie came painfully to her lips. "I don't think we ought to see each other again."

Kris felt her announcement like a powerful blow right to his solar plexus. It drove the breath from his lungs.

She was dumping him.

"I don't get it."

"My mother is very ill and I'm going to be very busy. I simply won't have time—"

"I could wait. You're under a lot of stress right now. I could help."

"No. Please don't make this any more difficult than it already is. Simply accept that I don't want to see you again."

A double dose of male ego and pride kicked Kris in the butt. He got the message, all right. His new image didn't mean squat. Even his money didn't give him any clout. Not with Joanna.

But that was all right, he tried to rationalize. Inherent in every project there was a certain risk. Sometimes the best-conceived elements of an advanced concept didn't fit when you put them together. He could live with that. He hoped.

Turning, he went out the door. After thirty-one years of achieving virtually every goal he'd attempted, it looked as though this time he'd have to live with failure.

He jammed his hands in his pockets. He didn't even know how to act. What was he supposed to do? He'd never felt so ignorant in his life. Or so torn by a pain that had no relief.

Standing in the pouring rain, he turned his face to the sky. Only the telltale warmth of his tears differed from the drops of rain that edged his cheeks.

Chapter Eleven

"Oh, drat it!" Agnes hobbled into the kitchen, her walker banging into the back of a chair. "This thing is more menace than help."

"You know the doctor said you need it for balance." Setting the casserole she'd prepared into the oven, Joanna pulled the chair out of the way to give her mother more room to get around the table. "He doesn't want you falling and breaking a hip next time."

"Using this thing is like dancing with a drunken sailor. I could do better on my own."

"It's only been a week since you fell." A week since Joanna had seen Kris, and still her heart felt like a stone in her chest. "The doctor thinks you're doing remarkably well." Far better than she was.

"Bah! I should be planting my bulbs now. You know how your father used to love daffodils in the spring."

"You could have been planting whatever you liked in your garden if you hadn't taken a header down the back hill. Honestly, Mother, why would you do something so—so…"

"Crazy?" Agnes supplied. "You'll learn when you get to be my age that sometimes you want to kick up your heels and feel young again. Your father and I…" Her voice caught.

A matching lump of longing crowded in Joanna's throat. "It's all right, Mother. Just be careful next time. I don't want to lose you."

Turning to the window, Agnes fussed with the plants on the sill. "I think Tyler watered these too much. I hope they don't get root rot. He should have been more careful."

Riding an emotional roller coaster, Joanna felt her chin tremble. "He was trying to help."

"Oh, I know, dear. It's just that I feel so useless. If I can't look forward to my daffodils, what can I look forward to?"

"Be patient, Mother." Time was bound to improve Agnes's mobility, just as time would heal Joanna's wounds. Soon the ache in her chest wouldn't be so severe when she passed the rental property and saw Kris's truck in the lot. Or even when the thought of him slipped unbidden into her mind. She would stop lying awake at night thinking about him. Dreaming about him. It was only a question of days or weeks—or years, she thought grimly—before she would get her life back in order again.

The doorbell rang. Before she could stop herself,

her breath caught on the hope that it might be Kris. But that wasn't possible. He'd stayed away for a week, at her request. There would be no reason for him to drop by now. More likely it was someone looking for Tyler.

"You get it, dear," her mother urged. "It would take me from now to Christmas to walk that far."

Drying her hands on a tea towel, Joanna went into the living room. When she opened the front door, she discovered Herbert Parkin on the porch. Wearing his London Fog raincoat and a dapper hat, he looked like a mature model for *GQ*. She returned his warm smile, fighting off the stab of regret that it wasn't Kris standing there in his place.

"I hope your mother isn't napping," he said.

"No, she's in the kitchen fretting about not being able to plant her daffodils for spring."

He held up a glossy brochure. "I have something that will take her mind off her troubles."

Curious, Joanna followed him into the kitchen. Her mother was sitting at the table. With easy familiarity, Herbert bent to kiss her.

"How are you, dear?" he asked.

"So testy I think I'm getting on my daughter's nerves."

"No, you're not, Mother—"

"I hate being an invalid," her mother insisted.

"I think I have the perfect prescription to cure your ills." He placed the brochure in front of Agnes. "A Mediterranean cruise. Athens. Crete. Istanbul. Twenty-one glorious days of being pampered."

"Oh, Herbert, I can't—"

"Mother can barely walk," Joanna interjected, wondering if Herbert had slipped into senility along with Agnes.

"It's an Easter cruise, my dears. By then Agnes will be so fit she'll be able to take on all comers at shuffleboard and win."

Agnes sputtered, though her eyes had begun to glitter with excitement. "But the Mediterranean? That's so expensive. I couldn't—"

"Naturally, you will be my guest." Sitting down, he covered Agnes's age-spotted hand with his. "I'd be more than happy to book two staterooms on the upper deck, the best available. Of course, I'm not a man to spend money unnecessarily, so I would be even more pleased if you would permit me to book only one room for both of us."

"Herbert!" Her cheeks colored and she tittered like a teenager. "Such talk! Whatever will Joanna think?"

Joanna choked back a laugh. "I think I'll go grade some test papers while you two work out your own sleeping arrangements." She rested her hand on Herbert's shoulder in a gesture of gratitude for brightening her mother's spirits. "Just be sure Mom doesn't come home pregnant. I'd have a devil of a time trying to explain that to Tyler."

She left the room to a duet of laughter. Her mother deserved all the happiness she could get, even if it was fleeting. Who knew, maybe with something positive to look forward to, her morale and health would improve substantially.

Less than an hour later, Herbert left, declining Joanna's invitation to stay for dinner.

"I don't want to tire your mother," he said. "She has enough to think about for now."

"You're sweet, Herbert." Joanna stood on tiptoe to kiss his cheek. "Thank you."

"I want you to know I intend to wed your mother as soon as she'll have me, though I don't think she's ready to broach the subject yet. I'd like that cruise to be our honeymoon trip."

Joanna was stunned. "I hope you understand— Mother isn't always... Her mind, well, sometimes she's a little eccentric..."

"She is *fun* to be with, my dear. However much I loved my wife, she was a very serious, driven individual. Agnes makes me smile. If she seems a little confused of late, I think it's because she simply hasn't recovered from the death of her husband. She's a woman who is capable of great love."

"Yes, that's true. But she's fallen once now, and with the concussion and all, that may mean—"

"If I could bask for only a year in that love, or even a single day, I would consider myself blessed." He brushed a kiss on Joanna's cheek. "Don't wear yourself out taking care of her. Agnes has more fortitude than most women half her age."

After Herbert left, Joanna went back into the kitchen, considering his comments. Her mother was at the table pouring over the brochure like a high-school senior studying a college catalog.

"Did you know I always wanted to see the Parthenon?" she asked without glancing up from the color photos. "And Turkish dancers? Whew, wouldn't your father have loved that?"

Joanna retrieved the salad makings from the refrigerator. "Yes, he probably would have liked that."

"Joanna?" Her mother's voice was tentative, her expression clouded. "Would it be awful if I went with Herbert?"

"Of course not. You deserve whatever pleasure you can find. And Herbert is a very dear man."

"I loved your father more than life itself."

"I know. And the last two years of his life were so hard on you. He was so terribly ill."

"I cherished every day he lived. *Every* day, no matter how sick he was. If it was my choice, I'd still be taking care of him. But now..."

Kneeling, Joanna wrapped her arms around her mother. She was more frail than she had been before the accident, her life somehow all the more precious. "I'd like for you to go with Herbert on the cruise, and I insist you have a wonderful time."

"You won't think I'm wicked?"

"Of course I will," Joanna exclaimed, laughing. "And I'll envy you."

"You wouldn't have to envy me if Kristopher hadn't vanished. Where is that young man? He only came to see me once at the hospital."

"He's busy, Mother." Busy making a life for himself after Joanna had rejected all he had offered. Not that he'd actually made a commitment, she realized. But there had been that wonderful house...and the look in his eyes. Surely he'd been making plans for the two of them—plans she had rejected before he'd even said the words.

Perhaps she should give Kris the same choice Herbert had made. What had been a devastating shortcoming in the eyes of Tyler's father was a gift of joy from Herbert's perspective. Intellectually Joanna could understand that difference. But in her heart she was terrified of a repeat of the rejection that had so wounded her during the most emotional time of her life—when she'd been pregnant and unwed.

Honesty demanded she tell Kris why she had been afraid to risk her heart again—the whole truth about her family and how she secretly harbored the desire to be equally flamboyant. That secret had been buried so deeply she had hardly recognized it herself. Perhaps it was Herbert's total acceptance of her mother's quirks that made Joanna hope another man could be just as accepting of her.

"Wow! What are you gonna do with all those bikes?"

At the sound of Tyler's voice, Kris looked up from fastening a miniaturized receiver to the frame of one of several pairs of bikes he had lined up across his shop. "The Foundation for the Junior Blind heard about our Smart Bike system and wanted to try it out with their kids."

"Hey, yeah. That'd be great." As he inspected the row of bikes, Tyler unconsciously twirled a football in his hands. His fleece jacket was a little too short in the arms and his socks were showing in the gap between his jeans and his ratty tennis shoes. The kid was growing as fast as a computer virus, Kris realized, an expensive process for a mother alone. He wished he could help out, but knew Joanna's pride wouldn't let her accept what she would view as a handout.

"Pete's already talking about entering a bunch of races next year," Tyler said. "He's totally jazzed. He figures if we train hard, by next spring we could place pretty high in our age group."

"You probably could." Kris's eyes followed the path of the football as Tyler tossed it in the air a few feet and caught it again with the easy grace of a natural athlete. "Say, how come you're not in school today?"

"It's Saturday, man. Did you lose track?"

"Yeah, I guess I did." For the past two weeks Kris had buried himself in his work. He didn't handle failure well and his only escape was to take on some new challenge. The trouble was, if it hadn't been for this unexpected bike project he would have felt very much at loose ends for the first time in his life.

Tyler circled the far side of the bikes. "So how come you and Mom aren't hanging around together anymore?"

"Things didn't work out," he hedged.

"You mean for you or her?"

"She's busy taking care of your grandmother. She doesn't have much time—"

"She sure has been acting dopey lately. You know, she yells at me for no reason, and sometimes it looks like she's been crying."

"Crying?"

Tyler examined the lacings on the football. "You think it's 'cause Grandma's gonna die?"

"I don't think so. I talked to Dr. Morgan last week. He seemed quite optimistic at the time."

Tyler hopped up to sit on a workbench and tossed the ball from hand to hand. "Well, if Grandma isn't gonna die, maybe Mom's upset because you haven't been over to see her lately."

Upset didn't begin to describe how Kris had felt. In the middle of a tornado of emotions would be closer to the truth. "It was her choice, son. She doesn't want to see me anymore."

"You mean she told you to get lost?"

"In spades."

"And you believed her?"

"Of course. She made her position crystal clear. A man isn't supposed to impose himself on a woman who doesn't want him around."

Tyler jammed the ball into his palm. "Oh, man, don't you know anything about girls? They tell you to take off when they totally want you to hang around. That's just the way they are."

"I don't think so, son." Though Kris could hardly count himself as an expert on the mental gymnastics of the opposite sex. Tyler could well know something he didn't.

"Man, what you gotta do is keep trying, that's what, like you made the team keep playing hard even when it looked like we were gonna lose. I mean, if you really like her 'n' stuff, you can't just give up."

"I like her." A lot. Kris's stomach knotted. No matter how hard he tried, he couldn't get Joanna out of his mind. Her image had shown up on his computer screen the other day. It was as if Internet had a direct link to his heart, until he blinked and the image dissolved into a thousand pixels of gibberish. Damn, not being with her hurt like hell.

"See, I figure my ol' man, the one who got Mom pregnant, was a quitter even if he was some big football jock at school. He ran out on both of us." Tyler hopped down to the floor again. "I didn't take you for a quitter, too, Kris. I thought..." His chin quivered. "Man, I thought..."

Kris couldn't remember ever being hugged by his father, but that was what he did with Tyler. He hugged the kid because he wasn't sure what to say and because probably the worst thing in the world was to grow up thinking your ol' man didn't love you. Maybe, in fact, that you weren't very lovable at all. And somehow, no matter how hard you tried, it was your fault.

"I love you, Kris. I thought maybe...I wanted you to be my dad."

Kris's throat tightened with emotion. "So you think maybe I ought to give it another shot with your mom?"

"If you want."

Kris inhaled the scent of the youngster, kind of sweaty and rank, and he wanted this boy to be his own. "Well, you're the expert on girls. What do you think would work best with her?"

Tyler lifted his shoulders in an awkward shrug. "I dunno. Something romantic, I suppose. She always gets all teary eyed over those mushy movies. You know, where they kiss 'n' stuff, and there're all those swoopy violins playing. It's really gross.''

"Ah." That didn't give Kris much of a clue, given the fact he wasn't into old movies, but he'd come up with something. Obviously, Tyler was counting on him. Besides, Kris had never been called a quitter in his life. That hurt. Because of his pride, he hadn't let himself realize he'd given up on the one thing in the world that was most important to him—Joanna.

"Look, man, I gotta go." Surreptitiously, Tyler swiped his knuckles across his eyes. "I'll see you around, eh?"

"I'll be here." Kris followed the boy to the open door of the workshop. "Hey, kid, let me have the ball a minute."

"Sure." Tyler tossed him the football.

"Now, go out for a pass. A long one." He figured a kid like Tyler, with all of his natural athletic ability, deserved a father who could at least throw a spiral pass.

Tyler jogged out onto the parking lot.

"Farther," Kris ordered, waving the boy back.

A little skeptically, Tyler kept on going.

When the boy was halfway across the property, Kris lifted a pass toward him. The trajectory arced across the parking lot, the ball spinning in a picture-perfect spiral until it landed in Tyler's outstretched fingertips. He pulled it in to his belly and held on tight.

"Way to go, Coach!" Tyler dodged, juking left and right as if avoiding a whole team of tacklers.

Kris grinned. "I'll talk to your mom, son." Just

as soon as he came up with an unbeatable concept, one she wouldn't be able to resist.

Monday holidays were a blessing.

Joanna had spent most of the morning in her classroom changing bulletin-board displays in preparation for the new unit she would introduce tomorrow. During the afternoon, she'd taken Tyler on a desperately needed shopping trip. How he'd outgrown his new school clothes so early in the year was beyond her. If she hadn't been afraid it would affect his health, she would cut back on his vitamins by half!

At least all the activity had kept her mind off of Kris—mostly.

Now that she was camped out in her bedroom with the lonely task of grading papers, thoughts of Kris kept inserting themselves in a most insistent way. She had to find an excuse to talk to him, and she wasn't at all confident of her welcome.

Undoubtedly she'd hurt Kris by sending him away so abruptly with little or no explanation. She wouldn't blame him if he was mad at her. Furious, in fact.

With a perverse twist of illogic, she wished the roof at the rental property would develop a leak and he'd have to come see her. Then she could apologize. And explain.

She leaned back in the chair and closed her eyes. The sound of a single violin drifted in through the window, and then another string instrument took up the harmony. Odd that a neighbor would be having a party on a Monday night, she thought. Unusual

music, too, since most of the neighbors preferred
hard rock to classical melodies.

A car door slammed. Guests arriving, she assumed. Vaguely she heard the buzz of conversation.

Setting the test papers aside, she strained to hear
what was going on. Her mother had gone to bed
early, and Joanna wouldn't want whatever was happening to disturb her. Tyler, as usual, was with his
friends watching Monday-night football.

She stood and peered out the window. Since her
room was at the side of the house, there wasn't much
to see—just a few pines silhouetted against the night
sky and the dark outline of the neighbors' house. It
didn't even look as if they were home.

Curiosity drove Joanna from the room. A strange
warmth filled with anticipation crept down her spine
and curled through her midsection. Who was out
there? she wondered. And why?

Tugging a heavy sweater on over her T-shirt, she
headed toward the front room. The music grew
louder, though still melodic and sweet, decidedly romantic in its mood and very close at hand.

She opened the door.

Kristopher Slavic, the picture of sophistication in
a dark tux, white shirt and bow tie, sauntered up the
steps toward her.

"Good evening," he said with a slight bow.

Her jaw went slack. "Hello." Looking past Kris,
she spotted a group of people in her front yard, each
producing beautiful classical music on their string
instruments. "Who are they?" And what on earth
were they doing on her lawn?

"The San Francisco String Quartet. They had the night off."

Surprised, Joanna raised her eyebrows. "And they decided to perform a concert here? Outdoors on a rather chilly night in Twain Harte?"

He looked full of himself. "I offered them triple their usual fee. Plus expenses, of course."

"Of course." Men with money did things like that, she supposed. "But why?"

Ignoring her question, he gestured toward the street. "That van's from the City Hotel. A take-out special. Pâté and escargot for appetizers, two kinds of wine, and you have a choice of chicken in a wine sauce or steak, medium rare, for the entrée. There's some fancy layer cake for dessert."

"You brought dinner?"

"So we'd have a little privacy, there's a tent from A-1 Rentals—"

"What?" Her head snapped around to follow his gaze to the far side of the yard.

"I asked you out to dinner the first time we met and you never said yes. So I figured it'd be smart to bring dinner to you."

"We're going to eat in a tent?"

"It's heated. They've promised me seventy-two degrees no matter how cold it gets tonight."

She choked back a laugh. "You're crazy!"

Taking a step closer, he framed her face with his hands. His breath was a warm caress across her cheeks. "I'm in love, Joanna. I'm not real good at this, and I'd appreciate it if you could cut me a little slack here. With practice, I'm sure I'll get it right."

The violins swelled to a crescendo. Joanna's heart did the same. "In love?"

"Yeah. Could we wait until we get into our little tent to discuss this in detail? The musicians are freezing their butts off and the cold makes their instruments go sharp. I promised them they wouldn't have to play long."

"So what's going to happen after they leave?"

"I've got a stereo set up and a tape. You'll never miss 'em."

Joanna didn't imagine so. Her only interest was in Kris and what he had in store for her this evening. "If I'd known this was a formal event, I would have dressed for the occasion."

"You look just fine to me." His gaze swept over her old sweater and worn jeans with so much masculine approval it made Joanna feel like a princess gowned in the finest silks and satins. Regally, he offered his arm.

As he escorted her to the brightly colored party tent, the musicians smiled at her knowingly. She flushed. Kris really was going to have to learn not to be so extravagant. Even a multimillionaire should spend his money with care.

As promised, overhead propane heaters had taken the chill from inside the tent. A table for two was set with a white cloth, candles and a huge bouquet of red roses that scented the air. Two waiters hovered near a second table holding several covered serving dishes. This had to be the most elegant take-out Joanna had ever seen. Pizza or Chinese was her usual style.

Kris seated her, then said to the waiters, "Thank you, gentlemen. I think I can take it from here."

With a bow, the staff departed. From a chilled bottle, Kris poured sparkling champagne into fluted glasses. Sitting down opposite her, he lifted one in a toast. "To you. And to us."

She sipped, the bubbles tickling her nose. "Why are you doing this when I was so mean to you? I'm sorry for what I said to you. But I did have my reasons. Though in retrospect they might not have been very good ones."

"Tyler said you'd been crying a lot lately."

"He talks too much, but he's very observant. I've been miserable."

"Me, too." Kris's long, tapered fingers looked both large and gentle on the fragile glass, and very masculine. Imagining them stroking her body with the same tender care brought a flush to Joanna's cheeks and an aching warmth to her midsection.

"Tyler also called me a quitter," Kris continued. "I figured I had to prove him wrong. Joanna, I—"

"Kris, before you say anything else I have something to tell you. Something important that may change your mind about what you want to say." Or at least what Joanna hoped he was here to say. "You see, I haven't been entirely honest with you."

The candlelight flickered, emphasizing the interesting angles and planes of his handsome face, his strong jaw and sensual lips. "Go on." He nodded.

"You never met my grandmother. She was..." *Crazy*, Nate had called her. "She used to do things that were a little unusual. Like decorating her house for Christmas in July. And collecting every bit of string that ever came her way. Miles and miles of string."

Joanna paused and waited for Kris to comment. To look horrified. Instead he remained silent.

"My father...well, you've seen how he amused himself. He made whirligigs of every possible shape and description."

"Yes, they're quite fascinating. I can understand why someone could get hooked on their aerodynamic characteristics."

He did? Clearly Kris didn't understand the implication of her confession. "Tyler's father thought the bizarre behavior of practically every member of my family probably had a genetic component. And that I carried that same ridiculous gene."

"Had he read a study to that effect?"

"No, not that I know of."

"Joanna, is there a point to you telling me this? I don't see anything particularly wrong with putting up Christmas decorations in July. And collecting string is pretty harmless. Whatever Tyler's father thought of all that doesn't have anything to do with us."

Perhaps Kris was being intentionally dense. "You've met my mother. There are times when she doesn't know where she is. Or she forgets my father is dead and talks about him as if any minute he's going to walk in the door for dinner. My goodness, you've seen how she dresses."

He looked genuinely perplexed. "What's wrong with how she dresses?"

"Haven't you noticed she has purple days and

apricot days and electric blue days? Why, her bizarre hair color alone should have given you a clue that she doesn't always have a solid hold on reality.''

His lips quirked in a half smile. ''She looks just fine to me.''

''She does?''

''I'm color-blind, Joanna. I guess I forgot to mention that.''

She stared at him, dumbfounded. ''But you knew, right from the start, that my eyes are blue. You said so.''

''I can tell the intensity of color, not the shade. Blue eyes tend to be less intense than brown, so I guessed.''

''Amazing. I didn't realize.'' Though perhaps she should have been more suspicious about his color perception when he recommended her mother to Percy as an interior decorator.

''I'm afraid it's a hereditary trait. My maternal uncle is color-blind, too.''

''A genetic flaw?''

''Yep. And if you dumped me because you're afraid you're going to do things that are a little quirky, then you ought to meet my family.''

''I met your sister and she didn't exactly approve of me. I doubt the rest of your academic family would be any more impressed than she was.''

''Hey, we've all got our personal foibles. My mother cooks dinner over a Bunsen burner—when she takes the time. Dad composes terrible limericks in Latin. If you think having peculiar family genes is awful, then I guess I ought to tell you goodbye because I'm color-blind.''

"That's ridiculous. Something like that doesn't affect how I feel about you."

Eyes darkening to a deep pewter that caught the candlelight, he moved a little closer to her. "How *do* you feel about me, Joanna?" His voice was deep and husky with traces of wanting and need.

"I..." She took a steadying breath. Now was the time for the truth, all of it. "I love you, Kris. I love you so much I'd never want to embarrass you or be a burden to you. And that's what would happen if I—"

"I don't much care what kind of genes you've got, because all of them look terrific to me."

"I inherited all of my grandmother's balls of string," she warned him. "Someday, when I have time, I'm planning to crochet them into tablecloths."

"That's fine with me."

"And next year I thought...well, I *liked* having Grandma's house decorated in July. It was fun. I plan to make it a family tradition."

"Great. I'll help you. We never did anything like that at my house." He leaned across the table and kissed her. Thoroughly. "Sweetheart, when I left Nanosoft I knew there was something missing in my life, but I didn't know what it was until I met you and your mother and Tyler. I want to be part of your life and I don't much care what color clothes you wear, now or twenty years from now, or how many balls of string you collect. I want to love you and be married to you and help raise your son."

Joy threatened to burst in Joanna's chest, but she held it in check.

He reached into the bouquet of flowers and produced a velvet box. Her eyes widened as he displayed a huge diamond ring. "Marry me, Joanna. Come live with me on top of the hill and watch a thousand sunsets from the back deck. Tyler is all any man could want in a son, but if you want to consider having more children, I can pretty well guarantee they'd love having Christmas in July."

"Tyler is growing up awfully fast," she conceded. Lord, she wanted Kris's babies, longed to see the replica of his beautiful smile on a child of her own.

"So we can decide later if we want children."

"You know I'm heavily in debt. The rental property—"

"I can handle it. The more write-offs the better, according to Percy. In fact, I can handle anything if you'll marry me. Please."

She closed her eyes, happiness nearly overwhelming her. "Yes," she whispered.

As Kris slipped the ring onto her finger, he said, "Tyler was right. A man shouldn't quit trying when something important is at stake."

She looked down at the ring and the way the candlelight caught the facets in a colorful rainbow. "I'm glad I have such a wise son."

"Pretty smart husband-to-be, too."

"A genius," she concurred.

Standing, he pulled her to her feet. Slowly, he dipped his head and claimed her lips with a kiss filled

with love and passion and sweet promises for the
future.

When he finally released her, Kris gazed intently
into her eyes and whispered, "Did you know, on
average, a married man lives six years longer than a
man who never marries?"

The corners of her lips quivered with the threat of
a smile. "Oh? Do I detect a little self-interest in this
marriage proposal?" she teased.

"Not at all. I'm simply thinking about how much
I'm going to enjoy every one of those six years and
every day leading up to them. And I'm going to start
enjoying them right now."

"So am I, my love. So am I."

Epilogue

Joanna stepped in through the front door and was struck again by the way the architect had managed to include the Sierra foothills as part of her home as much as he had the high, beamed ceilings and lushly carpeted areas. The view through the sliding glass doors at the back of the house gave her unending pleasure.

So did her husband.

"Kris, are you here?" she called. In the three months since they'd been married, she'd learned the presence of his truck out front didn't mean he would be waiting to greet her. He had such tunnel vision when he was working on one of his projects that he often didn't hear her arrive when she returned home after school.

Dropping her school papers and keys on the kitchen counter, she went in search of him.

His office was a maze of snaking electrical cables

that connected computers and assorted peripheral equipment to each other and the outside world. She came up behind him, slipped her hands over his shoulders and down his chest, and kissed him on top of the head.

"Hard at work, eh?" she said.

He typed a few keys to save the screen and caught her wrists. "Good day?" he asked, shifting so he could bring her head down to his for a kiss.

"The kids are always a little hard to settle down after a vacation. Easter week is no different."

"We got a postcard from your mother. Apparently they won a prize for the best costumes at some dinner dance on the cruise ship and she was a little embarrassed. She hadn't realized it was costume night and she was wearing her fanciest gown."

"Poor Mother. I hope Herbert didn't mind."

"I doubt it." Kris stood and took Joanna in his arms. "I love you," he said simply.

"I know. And I love you, too." She felt her smile building from the inside out, her contentment along with it.

He nuzzled the side of her neck with his lips, sending rippling waves of desire through her. "I went to the bookstore today."

"Really?" Her gaze slid to a stack of books on his heavily burdened desk.

Parenting for Beginners, What to Expect When You're Expecting, The First Year—

She swallowed a gasp. "I take it you're thinking of starting a new project?" One he'd no doubt focus all of his energies on, to her great pleasure.

"Well, we are getting up in years," he suggested. "Ancient."

"Then you agree we should take steps to provide Tyler with a younger sibling."

"Would I be so foolish as to argue with my husband?" she teased.

In an agile move, he lifted her in his arms and carried her toward their bedroom.

"Wait! We can't—I didn't mean right this minute." She sputtered as he placed her on their king-size bed. "What about Tyler? He'll be home for dinner any minute—"

"My dearest wife, you've forgotten your husband is a genius. In anticipation of putting all my recent book learning to good use, I cleverly suggested our son might want to spend the night at Pete's house."

"You did?"

"I did."

"This project may require more than one attempt, you know."

"I generally get things right the first time. But I'll be happy to repeat my performance as many times as you'd like."

She sighed. "That's very considerate of you."

With infinite care, he began removing her blouse, kissing each small bit of flesh as it was revealed. "Are you aware that, once fertilized, a human egg divides thirty-two times in a mere seventy-two hours?"

"Amazing." Her heart accelerating, her body responding with intimate familiarity to his touch, she arched up to him.

"And in the first year of life..."

He kissed her again and she lost all interest in the details he'd picked up from his research. She simply wanted to be his wife and the mother of his children. What wonderful celebrations they'd all have in July!

* * * * *

**Beginning in September
from Silhouette Romance...**

THE BRUBAKER BRIDES

a new miniseries by
Carolyn Zane

They're a passel of long, tall, swaggering cowboys who need tamin'...and the love of a good woman. So y'all come visit the brood over at the Brubaker ranch and discover how these rough and rugged brothers got themselves hog-tied and hitched to the marriage wagon.

The fun begins with
MISS PRIM'S UNTAMABLE COWBOY (9/97)

"No little Miss Prim is gonna tame me! I'm not about to settle down!"
—Bru "nobody calls me Conway" Brubaker
"Wanna bet?"
—Penelope Wainwright, a.k.a. Miss Prim

The romance continues in
HIS BROTHER'S INTENDED BRIDE (12/97)

"Never met a woman I couldn't have...then I met my brother's bride-to-be!"
—Buck Brubaker, bachelor with a problem
"Wait till he finds out the wedding was never really on...."
—the not-quite-so-engaged Holly Fergusson

And look for Mac's story coming in early '98 as
THE BRUBAKER BRIDES series continues, only from

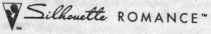

Silhouette ROMANCE™

BRU

Take 4 bestselling love stories FREE

Plus get a FREE surprise gift!

Special Limited-time Offer

Mail to Silhouette Reader Service™

3010 Walden Avenue
P.O. Box 1867
Buffalo, N.Y. 14240-1867

YES! Please send me 4 free Silhouette Romance™ novels and my free surprise gift. Then send me 6 brand-new novels every month, which I will receive months before they appear in bookstores. Bill me at the low price of $2.67 each plus 25¢ delivery and applicable sales tax, if any.* That's the complete price and a savings of over 10% off the cover prices—quite a bargain! I understand that accepting the books and gift places me under no obligation ever to buy any books. I can always return a shipment and cancel at any time. Even if I never buy another book from Silhouette, the 4 free books and the surprise gift are mine to keep forever.

215 BPA A3UT

Name	(PLEASE PRINT)	
Address	Apt. No.	
City	State	Zip

This offer is limited to one order per household and not valid to present Silhouette Romance™ subscribers. *Terms and prices are subject to change without notice. Sales tax applicable in N.Y.

USROM-696   ©1990 Harlequin Enterprises Limited

You've been waiting for him all your life....
Now your Prince has finally arrived!

In fact, *three* handsome princes
are coming your way in

ROYAL WEDDINGS

A delightful new miniseries by **LISA KAYE LAUREL**
about three bachelor princes who find happily-ever-
after with three small-town women!

Coming in September 1997—THE PRINCE'S BRIDE

Crown Prince Erik Anders would do anything for his
country—even plan a pretend marriage to his lovely
castle caretaker. But could he convince the king, and
the rest of the world, that his proposal was real—before
his cool heart melted for his small-town "bride"?

Coming in November 1997—THE PRINCE'S BABY

Irresistible Prince Whit Anders was shocked to
discover that the summer romance he'd had years
ago had resulted in a very royal baby! Now that
pretty Drew Davis's secret was out, could her kiss
turn the sexy prince into a full-time dad?

**Look for prince number three in the exciting
conclusion to ROYAL WEDDINGS,
coming in 1998—only from**

Silhouette ROMANCE™

DIANA WHITNEY

**Continues the twelve-book
series 36 HOURS in
September 1997
with Book Three**

OOH BABY, BABY

In the back of a cab, in the midst of a disastrous storm,
Travis Stockwell delivered Peggy Saxon's two precious babies
and, for a moment, they felt like a family. But Travis was a
wandering cowboy, and a fine woman like Peggy was better off
without him. Still, she and her adorable twins had tugged on
his heartstrings, until now he wasn't so sure that *he* was
better off without *her*.

For Travis and Peggy and *all* the residents of Grand Springs,
Colorado, the storm-induced blackout was just the beginning
of 36 Hours that changed *everything!* You won't want to miss a
single book.

Daniel MacGregor is at it again...

New York Times bestselling author

NORA ROBERTS

introduces us to a new generation of MacGregors
as the lovable patriarch of the illustrious MacGregor
clan plays matchmaker again, this time to his three
gorgeous granddaughters in

THE MACGREGOR BRIDES

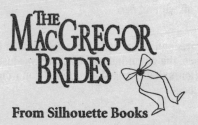

From Silhouette Books

Don't miss this brand-new continuation of Nora Roberts's
enormously popular *MacGregor* miniseries.

Available November 1997 at your favorite retail outlet.

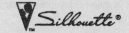

Silhouette®